7-6-03

To a dear friend
who has left her
footprints on my heart!
Your friendship and
Kindness has meant
so much to me. You
will be deeply missed.
I hope you will read
this and have a "good"
laugh every now & then.
Please stay in touch!
    I love you!

Never Kiss An Alligator On The Lips!

The Life And *Trying* Times of Boudreaux The Cajun

Volume 1

By

Curt Boudreaux, M.Ed.

Never Kiss An Alligator On The Lips!:
The Life And *Trying* Times Of Boudreaux The Cajun

Published by Synergy Press
Golden Meadow, Louisiana 70357

Published in the United States of America

Printed by Franklin Southland Printing
Metairie, Louisiana 70002

ISBN 1-889968-55-2

Cover design and special illustrations by Dolores Granger

Photo by Mike's Framing and Photography

CONTENTS

DEDICATION

This book is dedicated to

Derian Michael Theriot,

my lil podna,

who has brought so much love, laughter and joy

into my life.

May he grow up to value and appreciate his heritage

and enjoy life to the fullest.

ACKNOWLEDGMENTS

Special thanks and appreciation are expressed to the following people for their contributions:

Edmund Cappel, retired educator and my former English teacher, for editing the manuscript. After reading this piece of work written in dialect, he was probably thinking that little or nothing has changed since my ninth grade term papers.

Dolores Granger, neighbor and friend, for designing the cover and creating several of the illustrations. She is very talented and has great insight into the Cajun culture.

Norris Rousse, a friend who is well versed in Cajun history, for providing both written and verbal information.

Kelly Gaubert and others at Franklin Southland Printing, for their assistance in putting together the final product.

Senator John Breaux and **Dave Petijean** for their endorsements.

Mathew Bernard, Donald Bollinger, Sr., Dickie Borne, Sue Boudreaux, Deacon Sam Burregi, Chris Cedotal, Paul Champagne, Sylvia Champagne, Martha Collins, Mike Collins, Wayne Couvillon, Mary Jane Danigole, L.J. Dantin, Rene Daze', Patsy Landrus, Terry Landrus, Monsignor Francis Legendre, Joe Leonard, Janet Lococo, Carolyn Martin, Vince Melvin, C.J. Morgan, Ken Norton, Barbara Orgeron, Monica Pierre, Leroy Rybiski, John Serigny, Abby Shields, Steve Stall, Melvin Terrebonne, Tina Thomas, Willis Toups, Barry Uzee, Pat Vizier, Bill Webb and Tammy Zeringue for their stories and anecdotes. Their contributions made this project possible.

Testimonials

Never Kiss An Alligator On The Lips!

"Cajuns love to laugh, and they especially love laughing at themselves. Curt Boudreaux has captured the heart and soul of Cajun humor in **Never Kiss An Alligator On The Lips!** His stories are simply wonderful — and very funny."

Senator John Breaux
Washington, DC

"Your history of the Cajuns is one of the best I've read. These few pages give a good understanding of our origin. The jokes tell the whole story of the love of life and humor of us Cajuns. The Paul Revere story says it all. Keep on keeping on."

Dave Petijean, Cajun Humorist
Crowley, Louisiana

Introduction

Cajuns are known as hard working, fun-loving people filled with a zest for living—a joie de vivre, if you will. (joy of living) We love to eat, cook, hunt, fish, dance and tell jokes and stories.

Cajun cooking has become world famous because of the many talented chefs in Louisiana who have perfected this culinary art. Countless restaurants outside the state proudly tout Cajun dishes on their menus, but they are poor imitations at best. None can compare to the "real thing" found in the bayou land.

Stories and jokes abound about the escapades of Boudreaux, the Cajun, and his many friends — Shawee, Kymon, T-Boy, Gaston, Cowan, T-Brud and others in South Louisiana, the heart of Cajun Country. My purpose in writing this book is to share as many of these stories, anecdotes and sayings with you as I possibly can.

And just as with Cajun cooking, I believe these stories can best be told from the perspective of an authentic source, the "real thing", none other than ole Boudreaux himself. In addition to my last name and French heritage, what qualifies me to do this is simply my love of humor and desire to have fun as well the tenacity to sit down and put it in writing. How can you argue with that?

People in general do silly and, oftentimes, humorous things. Cajuns are no exception. This book will be an attempt to present some of these mishaps and see the funny side of life. Obviously, in most instances, there has been a gross exaggeration of facts and events, but they can still furnish a keen insight into the Cajuns' love for life and living. Their kindness, generosity and loving nature are unmatched.

Hopefully, no one will get "bent out of shape" or be offended by this book. Believe me when I say that it is not my intent to put anyone down. I am proud of my name and heritage, but I believe we should not take ourselves so seriously that we can't laugh at some of the things we say and do. The ability to laugh at oneself is essential to happiness in life and Cajuns possess the capacity to do just that. Laughter is the sunshine of the soul and a sign of a mentally healthy person. So I assume it is safe to say by the greatest stretch of the imagination that I'm attempting to promote mental health. Be that as it may, I simply want you to laugh and have fun as you read this book.

"In The Beginning" provides a brief history of the Cajuns' migration to Louisiana from Nova Scotia. Their strong beliefs, philosophy of life and desire to pursue a better way of living were instrumental in shaping their culture in their new homeland.

Some "You just might be a Cajun if" statements are strate-gically located at the beginning of each chapter throughout the book. These are specifically for those folks whose last name is not Boudreaux, Guilbeau, Fontenot or Robichaux but have a strong affinity for Cajuns and their way of life. They might also have a dog named Phideaux or even own a condeaux. These statements could help clarify the issue and perhaps solve this age-old mystery. On the other hand, you could simply trace your family tree to find out. But then, that wouldn't be as much fun, would it?

And of course the book wouldn't be complete without the famous, or should I say infamous, Boudreaux stories. These are legendary in Cajun country and have been collected from many and varied sources. They are meant to poke fun at all of us in general and no one in particular. They simply represent people. Some stories are original, and all are written in dialect to capture local flavor.

A glossary of terms concludes the book which will assist you in making "heads or tails" out of some of the words and phrases used. Learn them, use them, but be very careful — they are powerful and could easily get you into trouble. So get an interpreter if you need one!

As you begin your journey into the Cajun psyche, I leave you with the familiar and often used party yell, "Laissez Le Bon Temps Rouler!" (Let the good times roll!) I hope you pass yourself a good time as you move through these pages, sha. Shame on you if you don't!

Chapter 1

In The Beginning

In the spring of 1605, the French established a colony in Nova Scotia called Port-Royal. It was the first European settlement in North America, preceding Jamestown by two years and the landing at Plymouth by fifteen.

In 1671, a census revealed sixty-seven families at Port-Royal. The list was ladened with family names very similar to a modern day telephone directory in south Louisiana. From Aucoin to Daigle to Pitre to Thibodeaux.

The ownership of Acadian country changed hands a number of times during the succeeding years. England and France were in a constant state of war, with short periods of peace between conflicts. But the colony hung on and prospered in spite of this. By 1750, some families were entering their third generation of colonization.

The Treaty of Utrecht, signed in 1713, awarded Acadia's 2,500 inhabitants once again to England. The Acadians were informed that they would be required to swear an oath of allegiance to England in order to stay. They tried to have the wording changed but to no avail. Their basic concern was that in the continuing battle between England and France, they might be forced to bear arms against their Mother country. They protested for forty years.

But one day, a British commander acting without specific orders, took historic steps to clear the colonists from the land. He sent armed soldiers and ships to Nova Scotia with instructions to burn the villages. The order instituted one of the most talked about displacements in history.

It was a time of terror. Of more than 18,000 Acadians in that fateful autumn of 1755, over half disappeared forever. For those who survived, there was no more home for them in the land of their ancestors. They had no more country. They embarked for the unknown, without a backward glance, fleeing forever. Uprooted and hopeless, it was said that "all they had left was their hands and their prayers."

Each of the British colonies was forced to take some of the Acadians. None were forewarned of this except Massachusetts and Connecticut. They were unwelcomed guests since no provisions were made for their support.

Some were immediately rejected by their host governments and encouraged to return to Nova Scotia or France. Otherwise, they could fend for themselves in the British colonies. Some were even indentured in Georgia and the Carolinas. Many were permanently separated from their families.

Between 1764 and 1767, hundreds of Acadians immigrated to Louisiana. Arriving from Santo Domingo, Maryland and New York, these first Acadians were followed by many others. Their arrival in the colony marked the final stage of a tragic odyssey which had begun in Acadia and lasted for nearly a decade.

The long years of exile had neither broken their spirit nor undermined their ethnic unity. The circumstances of their early history had molded their character and thinking, so that now in Louisiana they were determined to preserve and continue their philosophy and way of life.

They were a fun-loving people with an unusual fondness for music, dancing, and above all, their beloved balls. On horseback, on foot, and by pirogue, they traveled as much as thirty to forty miles to attend these dances. At the sound of a couple of fiddles, young and old alike danced to their heart's content, usually well into the night.

Just as popular as the balls, but by far more practical, was the widely practiced custom of the boucherie. Taking turns to provide the animal to be slaughtered, neighbors and friends gathered for the day to cut and prepare the meats which were later divided among the participants. The original intent was to furnish people who did not have refrigeration with meat for immediate consumption, but in time the boucherie became a social occasion. It provided people with the opportunity to visit, exchange news and maintain contact.

Acadians were a close knit people. Their lives revolved around the family unit and the home. Families gathered during the evening to review daily activities, discuss the weather, crops and especially to reminisce. The Acadians were excellent storytellers and well versed in their rich history and folklore. They repeatedly related tales of their beloved Acadia, keeping the past alive for their children and grandchildren. These early Louisiana Acadians jealously guarded their religious and ethnic inheritance and left an indelible cultural pattern for many generations to come.

The word "Cajun" evolved from the Acadians themselves. They pronounced the word Acadian in French as "A ca jan" which eventually was shortened to "Ca jan." As the years passed, more and more people simply began saying "Cajun" as it is used today. It is often said in Cajun country that there are two groups of people in the world: Cajuns and those who want to be. Which group are you in, sha?

You just might be a Cajun if...

Watching Wild Kingdom on television inspires you to write a cookbook.

You think Ground Hog Day and Boucherie Day are the same holiday.

You sit down to eat boiled crawfish and your host says "Don't eat the dead ones" and you know what he means.

Your dog thinks the bed of your pickup is his kennel.

Chapter 2

Boudreaux On Animals & Hunting

Mistaken Identity

Boudreaux and Shawee were paddling through the marsh in a pirogue when an alligator surfaced and bit Boudreaux on the leg.

"Shawee, Shawee!" said Boudreaux excitedly. "An alligata done bit me on da leg!"

"Which one?" asked Shawee.

"May, ah don't kno!" said Boudreaux. "All dem darn alligata look alike ta me!"

Good Horse Sense

Boudreaux went to the dance, a fais-do-do, on his famous red horse one Saturday night. The music was playing and everybody was having a good time. Boudreaux was just dancing away with all the ladies. As it got to be twelve o'clock, he figured that Chlotilde might come looking for him so thought he'd better go home. He went outside to get on his red horse and, low and behold, he was back inside the dance hall in a flash.

"Stop da music!" shouted Boudreaux as he jumped onto the bandstand. "Ah wanna kno, me, who painted my red hoss green?"

A Texien sitting at a table said, "Boudreaux, I painted your red horse green!"

Boudreaux looked at him and said, "You! You da one dat painted my red horse green?"

The Texien stood up and was taller than Boudreaux even though Boudreaux was up on the bandstand. He said, "Yeah! It was me! I did it! What about it?"

"Well, sha, ah jis wanchu ta kno dat he dry and ready fo' da second coat," said Boudreaux sheepishly.

Going The Extra Mile

Boudreaux was driving to New Orleans when he saw a truck filled with monkeys stalled on the side of the road. He stopped and asked the guy if he could help.

The man said, "Well, I was taking these monkeys to the Audubon Zoo. Tell you what, I'll give you $20.00 if you take them for me."

"No prablum, sha. Ahm mo' den glad ta do dat fo' ya," said Boudreaux. He loads the monkeys in his truck and takes off for the zoo.

Three hours later Boudreaux is passing back and sees the same stalled truck still on the side of the highway. The man is frantically waving his arms for him to stop.

Boudreaux stops and asks the man, "May, wats da matta witchu? Watchu all excited abot?"

"I gave you money to take these monkeys to the zoo for me but you still have them in the truck. What are you up to?" said the man.

"Aw, dere's nutting ta worry abot," said Boudreaux. "Ah done already took dem ta da zoo. But ah had me a lil money lef ova from da twanny dolla so ah taut ah would give dem a treat and take dem ta da circus, too!"

Man's Best Friend

Boudreaux was walking in his neighborhood and saw Cowan with a dog.

"May ware ya got dat nice lookin' dog, you?" asked Boudreaux.

"Ah got it fo' my wife," replied Cowan.

"Huh, ah kno yo wife, me," said Boudreaux, "and ah kin tellya rat now, dat wudn't no bad trade non, sha!" exclaimed Boudreaux.

Dead Solid Perfect

Boudreaux was at the hunting camp with Shawee, Kymon and T-Brud. They were drinking beer and playing bouray at the kitchen table.

"Oh, Boudreaux," asked Shawee, "ya comin' hunt dem bear wit us in da mornin', you?"

Boudreaux, the excellent hunter that he is, replied, "Aw non. Ah tink ahm goin' go by mysef, me. Ah hunt mo betta dat way."

In the morning, when everyone else was waking up to go on the hunt, there was ole Boudreaux back from his trip with a big black bear. There was only one bullet hole on the bear, right between the eyes.

"Chooooo, you a good shot, yeah!" exclaimed Kymon who was leaving to make his hunt.

"Haw yeah! One shot. Dat's all ah need, me!" bragged Boudreaux. "Ah tolju ah wuz good."

Boudreaux's podnas came back later that day without a single bear. That night they once again went through the ritual of drinking beer and playing bouray. Kymon asked Boudreaux if he was going on the hunt with them in the morning.

"Aw non, sha," answered Boudreaux. "Ah hunt mo betta jis wit me."

In the morning the three hunters were leaving the camp as Boudreaux was returning. And, of course, he had another bear. This one, too, had only one bullet hole — right between the eyes.

"How ya do dat wit only one shot, you?" asked T-Brud. "Ya can't be dat good!"

The threesome went on their hunt and returned to the camp empty handed again.

The next morning Boudreaux returned a third time with a bear as his companions were leaving for their hunt. But this time, there were three bullet holes in the bear — one between the eyes, one in the left paw and one in the right paw.

T-Brud, seeing the three holes, exclaimed, "Uh huh! Ah knew ya couldn't do dat teree times in a row wit only one bullet! Ah knew ya wudn't dat good, me!"

Boudreaux calmly explained, "May non, sha. It ain't wat it look like, non. It only took me one shot. You see, it wuz purty dark when ah spotted dat bear. So ah turn on my bulleye (light) like dis and shine it in his eyes. Wen he saw da light, he put bote his hands ova his eyes ta cover dem. Dat's wen ah shot, me!"

Not Looking Good

Boudreaux decided to visit Gaston one Sunday afternoon. As they were walking on his farm, Boudreaux spotted Gaston's horse.

"Man, dat's da prettiest hoss ah naver did see, me," said Boudreaux. "How 'bout ya sell him ta me?"

"Haaaaaw, ah don't kno," said Gaston. "Ah done had him aver since he wuz a lil colt. And beside, he don't look so good."

"Pooyie, ah sho like dat hoss, me," said Boudreaux.

"Boudreaux, he jis don't look so good," chimed Gaston.

"Tellya wat ahm goin' do, me. Ahm goin' give ya a tousand dolla fo' him," pressured Boudreaux. "Ah want dat hoss bad bad."

"Okay," said Gaston reluctantly, "but ahm tellin' ya — he don't look so good, non!"

Monday afternoon Boudreaux came running up to Gaston's house and he was furious. He was so angry he was fit to be tied.

"Dat hoss ya sold me dere, Gaston, well, ah wantchu ta kno he's blind! And ah taut ya wuz my fran. How ya could do dat ta me!" exclaimed Boudreaux.

"Maaaaay, ah tolju teree times dat he don't look so good. Wat mo' ya want, you?" questioned Gaston.

Gator Guard

Boudreaux is sitting on his front porch and making very loud, strange noises. Gaston comes walking by and curiously asks, "you alrat, you?"

Boudreaux nods his head "yes" and continues making the weird sounds.

"Den how come ya screaming like dat?" asks Gaston.

"Cuz it keep dem alligata away," explains Boudreaux.

"Couyon, dey don't got no alligata round here fo' miles," says Gaston.

"May dere ya go. See how good it work!" says Boudreaux.

Deja Vu

Boudreaux and Kymon got T-Boy to fly them to Canada to go Elk hunting. It was a very successful trip with the two getting a total of six big bucks.

T-Boy came back to pick them up as had been arranged. They began loading the gear into the plane including the six elk.

T-Boy said, "Fellas, dis pleen kin take only fo' o' dem elk. Ya goin' hafta leave da udda two behind."

This caused Boudreaux and Kymon to get into a big argument with T-Boy. They had worked hard to get those elk and had no intention of losing them.

"Look, T-Boy," said Boudreaux, "da year befo' we had shot six and ya let us put dem all on board. And da pleen wuz da same model, capacity and arryting else — jis like dis one."

So T-Boy reluctantly allowed them to put all six on board. But when they attempted to take off and leave the valley, the little plane couldn't make it and they crashed in the wilderness.

Climbing out of the wreckage, Kymon asked Boudreaux, "Ya tink ya kno ware we at, us?"

"Ah belief so," answered Boudreaux. "Ah tink dis is abot da seem place ware T-Boy crashed da pleen las year!"

Truth Is A Virtue

Boudreaux offered to sell his dog to T-Boy for $10.00 and claimed the animal could talk.

"Please buy me," pleaded the canine to T-Boy. "Boudreaux doesn't feed me and he beats me with a whip. And I'm a really great dog. I was in the Gulf War and won the Distinguished Service Cross and the Purple Heart."

"Chooooo! Dat dog kin really talk!" exclaimed T-Boy. "May how come ya wanta sell him fo' only $10.00?"

"Sha, if dere's one ting ah can't stand me it's a liar." replied Boudreaux.

A Flying Miracle

Boudreaux was always bragging to his son, Junya, about what a great hunter he was. So Junya joined him on his next hunting trip just to see for himself if this was true.

They sat in a duck blind for a long time when one lonely water fowl winged its way through the sky. Boudreaux took aim and fired, but the bird continued to fly.

"Caaaaaw, Junya!" said Boudreaux. "Watchu see dere, son, is a miracle! Dere flies a dead duck!"

No Bull

Boudreaux and Shawee were going into the cattle business together. Needing to start-up their herd, they were lucky enough to see an ad in the newspaper that read, "Cow For Sale." They bought the cow and then realized that they needed a bull to breed her.

A few days later, Boudreaux was browsing through the newspaper and saw an ad, "Bull For Sale - $100.00." They decided to buy it but were uncertain how they would get the bull to their pasture. The bull's owner, Guilbeau, lived 75 miles away in the northern part of the parish.

Shawee decided to send Boudreaux to pick up the bull while he stayed home and tended to business. Arriving at Guilbeau's farm, Boudreaux paid him the $100.00 for their new acquisition. He now realized that no arrangements had been made for transporting the bull to his new home down the bayou. Boudreaux sat down and began to ponder a solution.

Guilbeau suggested that he send a telegram to Shawee in order to enlist his support and assistance. That sounded reasonable to Boudreaux, so he went down to the telegraph office.

"How much dat goin' coss me ta sand a message ta my fran Shawee," asked Boudreaux.

"Twanny-five sant a word," replied the clerk.

Boudreaux now realized that he spent all the money he had for the bull except for a quarter. He was in luck but what could he possibly say with only one word? After considerable thought, he sent the telegram to Shawee. Receiving the telegram, Shawee opened it but couldn't make heads or tails out of the word. Frustrated, he got in his truck and drove all the way to Guilbeau's farm.

"Oh Boudreaux! Wat's da matta witchu? Ya sand dat telegram dere wit only one word on it dat din make no sanse atall!" exclaimed Shawee.

"May watchu mean it din make no sanse?" asked Boudreaux.

"All ya had on dat paper dere wuz da one word — 'comfortable'. How ahm posta kno wat dat mean, me?" inquired Shawee.

"Couyon!" exclaimed Boudreaux. "It's as pleen as da big nose on yo face, yeah. Ah wuz jis tellin' ya ta 'come fo' de bull' — and you did!"

Music To His Ears

Boudreaux's son, Junya, was practicing his violin lesson in the house, while out on the porch Boudreaux was playing with the family dog. As Junya scraped away on the violin, the dog howled dismally.

Boudreaux stood it as long as he could, then poked his head in the open door and shouted, "Sha Lawd, Junya! Can'tchu play someting dat dog don't kno?"

Cajun Delight

Boudreaux and T-boy were hunting at the camp for the weekend. Suddenly, they saw this huge UFO land in the marsh. They didn't have a clue what it was.

"May wat's dat?" asked T-boy as the little green creatures came out of the spacecraft.

"Ah don't kno, me," replied Boudreaux as he aimed his gun, "butchu betta hurry back ta da camp and put some rice on cuz we got us some suppa tonite!"

Doggone Right

Boudreaux and Cowan were sitting on the porch at the camp one evening trying to decide on what they would do the next day.

Said Cowan, "You kno, Boudreaux, if ah knew fo' sho dat ah could kill me some duck tamorra, ahd go down ta da lake rat now, me, and sleep in da blind tonite."

Boudreaux replied, "May, Cowan, ya don't gotta go ta da lake ta see fo' yosef, non. Me dere, ah kin sand my dog, Phideaux, ta scout it out fo' us. He's smart, yeah."

So Boudreaux commanded Phideaux to go find out if there were ducks in the lake.

On his return a few minutes later, Boudreaux asked, "Hey, Phideaux, dey got some duck in dat lake, dere?"

Phideaux immediately barked five times which prompted Boudreaux to say, "May, ya see dere, Cowan. Dey got five duck in dat lake."

Not completely believing, but still curious, Cowan grabbed his gun and went down to the lake. Upon his return with five ducks, Cowan begged Boudreaux to sell him the dog. After much discussion and a few beers, Boudreaux agreed to sell Phideaux to Cowan. Needless to say he was delighted with his new acquisition.

Several weeks later Boudreaux met Cowan at the Hubba Hubba and asked, "Hey, Cowan, how's my ole dog Phideaux doin'?"

Cowan replied, "Ah got some bad news, me. Ahm sorry ta say dat ah had ta shoot him. Dat dog wuz good fo' nuttin', him."

Boudreaux was shocked and couldn't believe his ears. He exclaimed, "Cowan, you crazy, you? Dat wuz da bess dog ah naver did see, me, and you went and shoot him? May watchu do dat fo'?"

Cowan said sadly, "Ah did jis like you, me. Ah sant Phideaux ta da lake ta see fo' some duck but wen he come back he naver would bark. He - wouldn't - tell - me - a - ting! All he did, him, was jis sit dere wit a stick in his mout, shakin' his head back and fort like he wuz havin' a fit!"

"Couyon!" exclaimed Boudreaux. "He wudn't havin' no fit, him. He wuz jis telling ya dat dere wuz mo' duck in dat lake den ya kin shaka stick at!"

Doing What Comes Naturally

Boudreaux and Gaston were bear hunting in Alaska. Since this was not Boudreaux's first trip, he thought he would offer some advice to his podna.

"Gaston, if one o' dem bears git close ta ya, all ya gotta do is run like crazy," counseled Boudreaux. "And if he git too close, dere, turn aroun', grab a handful and trow it in his face."

"A handful?" asked Gaston. "A handful o' wat?"

"Don't worry, sha," said Boudreaux. "When da time come it goin' be dere!"

Never Kiss An Alligator On The Lips

"Boudreaux, lemme give ya some good advice, sha," said Shawee. "Don't naver kiss an alligata on da lip."

"May how come? asked Boudreaux.

"Cuz it's cold and it's wet," answered Shawee.

Boudreaux looked at him and said, "May, dat's da seem kind ah git at home, me — 'cept dey ain't wet!"

You just might be a Cajun if...

You shut down the entire town, including schools, for the opening day of squirrel season.

You have a son named Joe but spell it Jeaux.

Your children's favorite bedtime story begins, "First you make a roux..."

Your school teaches you that the four basic food groups are boiled seafood, broiled seafood, fried seafood and beer.

Your high school band's rendition of the national anthem begins, "Jambalaya, crawfish pie, file' gumbo..."

Chapter 3

Boudreaux On Education

Making The Grade

For the third straight nine weeks, Boudreaux's son, Junya, brought home a terrible report card. After reading it over, Boudreaux cringed and then signed it with an "x."

"May Poppa, how come ya done dat?" asked Junya.

"Cuz, sha," replied Boudreaux, "Ah sho don't want dat teacha ta tink dat annybody wit some grade like dat gotta daddy who kin read and wrat!"

Bird Legs

Boudreaux's nephew was in college and needed a small, two-hour course to fill out his schedule. The only one that fit in was a course in wildlife zoology. After just one week, the professor gave the class a test. He passed out a sheet of paper divided into squares. In each square was a carefully drawn picture of some bird legs — no bodies, no feet — just legs. The test asked the students to identify the birds from their legs.

Boudreaux sat and stared at the test and got more and more angry. Finally, he stomped up to the front of the classroom and threw the test on the teacher's desk.

"Dis is da most stoopidest tess ah aver took, me!" declared Boudreaux.

The teacher looked up and said, "Young man, you have just flunked this test. What's your name?"

Boudreaux pulled up his pants exposing his legs and replied, "You tell me, sha!"

31

Foreign Languages

Ole Boudreaux was quite an athlete in high school. But when he got his report card at the end of the first nine weeks, he had to give his coach the bad news.

"Hey, coach," said Boudreaux. "Ah got someting ta tellya. Ah ain't goin' be able ta play futball no mo dis year, non."

"Why?" asked the coach.

"Cuz ah ain't goin' be aligible. Ah failed French, me," said Boudreaux.

"But Boudreaux, how could you possibly fail French? You can speak it!" said the coach.

"Maaaaay, ah talk Anglish, me, but ah failed dat, too, yeah!" replied Boudreaux.

The Angle Of The Dangle

As Shawee was walking down the road, he met up with Boudreaux who was carrying a very long bamboo fishing pole and a yardstick. They stopped, talked awhile, and then Boudreaux stood the pole straight up in the air and attempted to reach the very top with the yardstick. Seeing that it wouldn't work, Shawee yanked the pole from him, layed it on the ground and measured it.

"Dere ya go, sha," said Shawee. "Da pole is twelve feet long."

"You stoopid, yeah you!" said Boudreaux. "Ah don't wanna kno how long da pole is, me. Ah wanna know how high it is!"

Continuing Education

Boudreaux and T-Boy were working at a construction site when a car with diplomatic plates pulled up. "Hablan ustedes Espanol?" the driver asked. The two just stared at each other.

"Sprechen sie Deutsch?" the driver tried. Boudreaux and T-Boy looked at each other even more puzzled.

"Parlate Italiano?" Still no response from the two Cajuns. Finally, the man threw up his hands in disgust and drove off.

T-Boy said, "Ya kno, Boudreaux, maybe we ought ta learn one o' dem foreign language, us."

"Huh, may how come?" asked Boudreaux. "Dat guy dere knew teree o' dem and it din do him no good!"

Math Magic

Boudreaux's son, Junya, was failing math. He and Chlotilde tried everything from tutors to hypnosis, but with no luck. Finally, with the encouragement of Shawee, Boudreaux decided to enroll him in a private Catholic school.

After the first day, Boudreaux and Chlotilde were surprised when Junya walked in after school with a stern, focused and very determined expression on his face. He went right past them, straight to his room, where he quietly closed the door.

For nearly two hours he toiled away in his room with math books scattered about his desk and on the floor. He emerged just long enough to eat some gumbo and potato salad. He quickly cleaned his bowl, went straight back to his room, closed the door and worked feverishly at his studies until bedtime. This pattern continued nonstop until it was time for the first quarter report card.

Junya walked in with his report card, laid it on the supper table and went straight to his room. Boudreaux cautiously opened it and, to his surprise and amazement, saw an "A" under the subject of math. Overjoyed, he and Chlotilde rushed into Junya's room, thrilled at his remarkable progress.

"Tel me, son, wat made da difference? Wuz it da nuns dat did it?" inquired Boudreaux.

Junya only shook his head and said "no."

"Wuz it da one-on-one tutoring?" asked Boudreaux.

"No," answered the youngster.

"Da peer-mentoring?" quizzed Boudreaux.

"No," replied Junya.

"Da textbooks?" questioned Boudreaux.

"No," responded Junya nonchalantly.

"Da teachas?" tried Boudreaux.

"No," said the student.

"Da curriculum?" asked a frenzied Boudreaux.

"Nope," retorted Junya.

"Den wat?" blurted Boudreaux.

"Well," explained Junya, "on da furst day wen ah walk myself trew da front door o' dat skool and ah seen dat guy dat dey nailed ta dat big 'plus sign', ah knew rat den and dere dat dey meant bidness, dem!"

No Ivy League Scholar

Boudreaux and Chlotilde were vacationing in the northeast. They had heard so much about Harvard being such a fine institution and wanted to visit it while in Massachusetts. They were in awe of the beauty and tradition as they strolled the campus. Caught up in the moment, Boudreaux decided that he wanted to go to the school library to find out more about this historical place. Not knowing where it was located, he stopped an approaching student.

"May ware's da liberry at?" asked Boudreaux innocently.

"Such atrocious English!" answered the snobbish student. "Any person with breeding and education would not think of ending a sentence with a preposition!"

"Okay den, ware's da liberry at, idiot?" asked Boudreaux again.

Courage In Action

Boudreaux was trying to educate a Bostonian on the valor and courage of the Acadians who left Nova Scotia fighting all kinds of odds and hardships. He related their struggles with disease and oppression. He also told him how the Acadians finally settled in Louisiana and became known as Cajuns.

"Sha, dey wuz some real heroes dem Cajuns, yeah!" boasted Boudreaux. "Ah betchu naver had nutting so brave like dat in Boston, you."

"Did you ever hear of Paul Revere?" asked the Bostonian.

"Paul Revere?" queried Boudreaux. "May, dat's not da guy dat ran fo' help, him?"

Poor Excuse

"Junya! Come here, boy!" yelled Boudreaux.

"Watchu want Poppa?" asked Junya as he responded to his daddy's call.

"Ah got dis letta here from da prancipal o' yo skool," answered Boudreaux. "He wanna kno abot all dem 'cuses dere wen you din go ta skool."

"May like wat, Poppa?" asked Junya.

"Don't play dum wit me, non, boy. Ah din git outa da pirogue yestiddy, non. Ahm talkin' abot dese rat here!" said Boudreaux excitedly as he begins to read them.

'My son Boudreaux is unda da dockta's care and shouldn't take P.E. taday. Pleez execute him.'

'Pleez axcuse Junya from P.E. fo' a few days cuz yestiddy he fell outa da tree and misplace his hip.'

'Pleez axcuse Junya from skool las Friday cuz he had loose vowels.'

'Pleez axcuse Junya fo' being absent yestiddy. He had diarrhea and his boots leak.'

'Pleez axcuse Junya fo' being absent cuz he wuz sick and ah had him shot.'

'Pleez axcuse my boy from skool cuz he had a cold and could not breed well.'

'Junya wuz absent Desamba 11-18 cuz he had da feva, sore troat, haidache and upset stomach. His sista wuz sick, too, wit da feva and da sore troat. His brudda, dere, had a low grade feva and he ache all ova, him. Ah wudn't in da bess o' healt mysef me nedda. Dere must be someting goin round cuz his poppa even got hot las nite.'

"And den ya had da gall ta sign my 'x 'on all o' dem. Dat's da most worstest part, yeah," said Boudreaux. "You in fo' a good butt whipping now boy. Watchu gotta say fo' yosef?"

"Not too much, Poppa, 'cept dat a po' axcuse is mo' betta den none atall!" replied Junya.

A Hard Lesson

"You kno, Kymon," said Boudreaux. "Ah tink ah finely undastand, me, how da state lottry hep aducation."

"Aw yeah?" said a quizzical Kymon.

"Dat's rat," said Boudreaux. "Arrytime ah buy a losing ticket dere, ah git a lil bit mo' smarter, me!"

You Can't Fool Me

Boudreaux had gone to Ville Platte on business and stopped at a restaurant. He paced up and down in front of it, glancing impatiently at the door. Inside, the cashier deduced that he was anxious to come in but something was holding him back. When the cashier had a free moment, he went outside and asked Boudreaux if there was anything he could do.

"No, tank you," said Boudreaux. "ahm jis waiting fo' da restrunt ta open."

"Why, it is open, sir," explained the cashier.

"Don't try ta fool me, non, sha," said Boudreaux. "Ah kin read, yeah, me. It say on da door rat dere, jis as pleen as da day, 'Home Cooking.'"

A Mind Is A Terrible Thing To Waste

Boudreaux saved and sacrificed a long time in order to send Junya to college. After being away for almost a year, he came home for spring break.

"Son, ahm mighty prod o' you fo' goin' ta college, yeah," said Boudreaux. "Wat kinda classes you taking ova dere anyhow?"

"English, Latin, Trigonometry and History," answered Junya.

Boudreaux wanted to find out if he was spending his money well and getting his money's worth. So he said, "Talk some Latin fo' me, son."

Junya responds with, "Ego Carpe Diem. It means 'Ah seize da day'."

Boudreaux thinks to himself, "Ah din go ta college, me, but ah tink it should be 'Ah see da day'."

He decides to try another subject. "Speak some trigonometry fo' me, son," urged Boudreaux.

"Poppa, ya don't 'speak' trigonometry," said Junya.

Boudreaux got very upset. "Look, ahm spanding a whole lotta money ta sand ya ta skool. If ah say speak trigonometry, den ya betta speak trigonometry, boy!" chided Boudreaux.

"Okay, ahm goin' give it a try," said a discouraged Junya. "Pi r square." (pie r square)

Boudreaux got very mad and rapped Junya on the head. "Afta all dat money ah spant ta sand ya ta college, you mo' dummer den aver, you. Pie are round, boy! Cornbread are square!"

You just might be a Cajun if...

When launching your boat at the dock you yell — LAUNCH — and everybody knocks off for a sandwich and a Barq's root beer.

You use a No. 3 washtub to cover your lawnmower or outboard motor in your back yard.

You use two or more pirogues to cover your newly planted tomatoes to protect them from a late frost.

The horsepower of your outboard is greater than that of the motor in your car.

Chapter 4

Boudreaux On Fishing

Creative Fishing

The game warden was making his rounds in the marsh when he began hearing loud explosions. He turned his boat in the direction of the noises and saw another boat in the distance. As he approached, he recognized the boat's occupant. It was none other than ole Boudreaux.

"Boudreaux," said the game warden, "what's making all these loud explosions?'

Boudreaux answered, "Maaaaay, ahm fishin', me."

"Fishing?" asked the game warden. "How can you possibly be making that kind of noise by fishing? Besides, you don't even have any fishing gear in your boat."

"It's a new way ah done learned ta catch dem spackle trout," said Boudreaux. "May, lemme show ya. Ah take me dis stick o' dynamite, ah light it, den trow it in da wata — like dis. Booooom! Wen it blow up, all da fish fly up in da arr and den fall in da boat. Den ah scoop'em up and put'em in my ice chest."

"Boudreaux, you can't do that," said the game warden. "That kind of fishing is illegal. I'm going to have to arrest you."

Boudreaux leaned over, picked up a stick of dynamite, lit it, tossed it to the game warden and said, "Now, sha, you goin' talk or you goin' fish?"

Thanks But No Thanks

Boudreaux, Shawee and T-Boy were fishing in Catfish Lake. Suddenly, they saw a figure walking on the water approaching their boat.

Boudreaux asked in a shaky voice, "Who, who you are, you?"

"I'm Jesus," said the man on the water.

"May, you don't tink we goin' belief dat jis cuz you say so. You gotta sho us a miracle ta prove dat," Boudreaux told him.

T-Boy said, "Hey, ah kno wat. Ah got me dis shoulder dat ah hurt wen ah wuz a lil boy. If you really Jesus, go 'head and cure it."

Jesus walked up to him and touched his shoulder.

T-Boy shouted, "Chooooo man, all da peen is gone! It's a miracle fo' sho!"

"Hummmm! You gotta do mo den dat ta convince me," said Boudreaux.

So Shawee said, "Hey, ah kno wat, me. Ah got dis elbow dat ah hurt playing futball at Sot Lafourche High School. Pooooo! It hurt bad, bad, yeah. It even hurt me wen ah fish. See if ya kin make it well, you."

Without saying a word, Jesus reached over and touched Shawee's elbow.

"Caaaaaw!" exclaimed Shawee moving his elbow all around. "It done naver felt dis good, non! Dat's sho nuff a miracle, yeah!"

Jesus then looked at Boudreaux and started walking towards him. Boudreaux quickly leaned back, put both hands in the air and shouted, "Haaaaaw non, don't touch me, sha! Ahm on Workman's Comp, me!"

Gold Fish

Boudreaux and Cowan decided to go on a fishing trip at a resort in North Louisiana. They rented all their equipment: the rods, reels, boat and even a cabin in the woods. They spent a small fortune on this outing.

They went fishing the first day with much anticipation, but didn't catch anything. The same thing happened the second day as well as the third. It went like this until finally on the last day of their vacation, Boudreaux caught a small fish. They were really discouraged and depressed.

Cowan looked at Boudreaux and said, "You realize dat dis one lousy fish coss us fifteen hundred dolla?"

"Sha Lawd, den good ting we din catch mo' den dat well!" exclaimed Boudreaux.

X Marks The Spot

Boudreaux and Shawee once again went to a resort in North Louisiana for a fishing trip. They rented a boat, got all the bait they needed, and left. They tried all the good spots the guide had told them about but had no luck. Not a single bite!

"May sha, dis is some ridiculous, yeah," said Boudreaux. "We been here all day and din git not one bite, us. Let's try one mo' spot. If we don't catch nutting dere, we goin' back ta da cabin, us."

They moved to another part of the lake and, lo and behold, started catching fish nonstop. They caught their limit and more.

"Quick, Boudreaux, pass me dat piece o' chalk ova dere," said Shawee.

"Watchu goin' do wit dat?" asked Boudreaux as he handed him the chalk.

"Maaaaay, ahm goin' mark dis spot on da side of da boat so dat da next time we come out here we kin remember ware we caught all dese fish," replied Shawee.

"Dat's da most stoopidest ting ah naver did hear, me!" said Boudreaux. "How you kno we gonna git da seem boat next time, Couyon?"

Launch Time

Boudreaux and T-Brud went to Minnesota to do some ice fishing. They stopped at a little store on the side of the road and asked the clerk where they should go. He informed them that there was a frozen lake just across the road and that he could sell them the bait and ice picks needed to break the ice. An hour later Boudreaux went back to the store to buy more ice picks.

"Gimme all da ice pick you got dere, sha," said Boudreaux.

"You're catching a lot of fish?" asked the clerk.

"Catching alota fish? Ah — guess — not!" replied Boudreaux. "We din even launch da boat yet!"

Going My Way?

Boudreaux owned a charter boat business that took anglers out in the Gulf for big-game fishing. As they cruised further out into the Gulf, they passed a deserted island, and the anxious fishermen were taking in the sights.

Suddenly, one of the fishermen pointed excitedly to the shore where a ragged, bearded man was running up and down, waving wildly.

"Who on earth is that?" he asked Captain Boudreaux.

"Ah dunno, me," said Boudreaux "but he sho like ta see me cuz he wave and scream like dat arry time ah pass dis way!"

Easy Guess

Boudreaux and T-Boy had been fishing in Catfish Lake. As they pulled their boat from the water at the dock, a Texien was launching his in preparation for an afternoon of fishing.

"How are they biting?" he asked.

"Uhhhhh, not too hot fo' dis time o' da year but we got us a few anyhow, yeah," answered Boudreaux.

"How about a wager?" challenged the Texien. "If I can guess how many fish you have in your ice chest, will you give me one?"

"Huh, ahm goin' do mo' betta den dat, me." said Boudreaux. "If ya kin guess how many fish ah got, sha, ahm goin' give ya bote o' dem!"

The More The Better

Unloading a huge, record-breaking redfish at the dock, an angler met Boudreaux whose catch consisted of 12 small, questionably legal, speckled trout.

"Hello," said the man as he carefully laid down his fish and waited for a comment.

Boudreaux stared for a few seconds then calmly responded, "Jis caught one, huh sha?"

This Bud's For Us

Boudreaux and Kymon were fishing in Catfish Lake when they saw a corked bottle floating by the boat.

"Dere's someting in dat bottle, yeah," said Kymon. "Watchu tink it is?"

"May ah don't kno but ahm sho gonna find out in a hurry, me," answered Boudreaux.

Boudreaux scooped the bottle out of the water and pulled out the cork. There before him appeared a genie. Boudreaux was startled.

"Sha, Lawd. Who you are, you?" asked a visibly shaken Boudreaux.

"I am a genie and I will grant you one wish — anything your heart desires," responded the genie.

"Maaaaay, ah taught dem genies is posta grant teree wishes, me. How come ya only give one, you?" inquired Boudreaux suspiciously.

"Well, you see, I am an apprentice and am learning how to be a full-fledged genie. So the Master Genie only allows me to grant one wish to see how well I do. Therefore, I will give you anything you ask," said the genie.

Boudreaux and Kymon went into deep thought trying to take full advantage of this golden opportunity.

After awhile Boudreaux said, "Ah kno wat, me. Ah wanchu ta turn all da wata in dis lake ta Budweiser beer."

"Haaaaaw yeah, dat's a good idear, sha!" exclaimed Kymon. "All da beer we want and fo' free, too!"

"Very well," said the Genie, "your wish is my command."

And with the snap of a finger — poof! — as far as the eye could see, all the water turned into Budweiser beer.

"It don't git no betta dan dis, non, sha!" exclaimed Kymon.

"Yeah ya rat, Kymon," said Boudreaux. "But ah tink we mita mess up, us."

"May watchu mean, you?" asked Kymon.

"Sha Lawd, now we gotta pee in da boat!" explained Boudreaux.

Silent Shots

Boudreaux and Shawee were fishing in Catfish Lake when they encountered trouble with the motor. They tried everything they knew but it still wouldn't start. Looking around, they saw no other boat in sight to lend assistance.

"You kno wat?" said Shawee. "Ah wuz always told, me, dat if ya have some trouble wit yo boat dat you jis shoot teree times in da arr and wait. Den somebody gonna come quick, quick."

"May we kin try dat, yeah," said Boudreaux as he fired three shots in the air. They waited but no one came. Boudreaux fired three shots again but still they were alone.

He continued for forty-five minutes — shooting, waiting, shooting, waiting until finally Boudreaux said, "Ya kno Shawee, if somebody don't come in a hurry, dere, ahm goin' run outa dem arrows purty soon, yeah!"

A Flying Miracle

You just might be a Cajun if ...

You learn to play bouray the hard way, by holding yourself up in the crib.

Any of your dessert recipes call for jalapenos.

You take a bite of 5-alarm chili and reach for the Tabasco.

You think boudin, hogshead cheese and Bud are a bland diet.

Chapter 5

Boudreaux On Gambling

All In The Game

One of Boudreaux's uncles was a Catholic priest. Father Boudreaux, a minister and a rabbi were playing bouray in the rectory. Before too long this card game became very intense and competitive. They began playing for money, big money, and the game soon got out of hand. A concerned neighbor called the police. The officer began his investigation by questioning the clergymen.

He asked the rabbi if he was gambling. The rabbi looked up toward heaven and said silently, "I'm going to have to deny it. It would look too bad for my people if this became public knowledge. I can't take that chance." So he answered, "No, officer. I was not gambling."

The policeman then asked the minister if he was gambling. The minister looked up to the sky and said to himself, "God, please forgive me because I'm going to have to say no. This would create such a scandal in my church, and I don't want to cause the congregation any embarrassment. I'll gladly take any punishment you see fit." So he, too, answered, "No sir. I was not gambling."

Then the cop looked at Father Boudreaux and asked, "Father, were you gambling?"

Father Boudreaux shrugged his shoulders, put his hands in the air and asked, "May sha, wit who?"

Dead Give-a-way

Boudreaux was playing bouray with Kymon, T-Boy, Shawee and his dog, Phideaux, at the Hubba Hubba. A Texien came in and immediately noticed the dog playing cards. He was impressed and amazed to see how good the dog was. When he commented on this, Boudreaux said in disgust, "He ain't dat smart non, sha. Arrytime he git a winning hand dere, he wag his tail!"

Wasteful Spending

Boudreaux was known as one of the cheapest guys in town. People were amazed that he looked so unhappy even after winning the eight million dollar lottery jackpot.

"Boudreaux, you a rich man now. How come ya look so sad, you?" asked Cowan.

Answered a dejected Boudreaux, "It's dis sacond ticket. Why in da world ah bought dat, me, ahm naver goin' kno!"

Winner Wants All

Early Monday morning Boudreaux drove to the Louisiana Lottery Headquarters in Baton Rouge to collect his winnings.

"Oh, beb," said Boudreaux to the clerk. "Ah got me da winning lottry ticket, and ah come ta git my money — all eight million dolla."

"Well, Mr. Boudreaux," explained the clerk, "we don't give the money all at one time. We'll pay you four hundred thousand dollars a year for the next twenty years."

"Haw non, sha!" said Boudreaux. "Ah sho ain't goin' wait no twanny years fo' my money, me. Ah won it fare and square and ah want all o' it rat na!"

"I'm sorry, sir," said the clerk, "but that's not the way it works."

"Well den, beb," said a furious Boudreaux, "if ya can't gimme all my money taday, den here is yo ticket and you kin gimme back my dolla!"

Lucky Seven

Boudreaux and Gaston got a job at a casino in Biloxi and were working the dice table.

"Look Boudreaux," said Gaston, "my sista's comin' in tonite, and she's bringin' a fran wit her. Man, talk abot a gooood lookin' woman!"

"May, ah kin hardly wait ta see her, me," said Boudreaux. They anxiously awaited her arrival, and at 9:00 o'clock in walks this gorgeous woman. It was cold outside so she had on a full length coat. She walked up to the table and said, "Give me the dice! Give me the dice! I'm ready to roll and win all the money!"

She grabbed the dice, rolled them around in her hand, blew on them and then let them fly across the table. As she threw she yelled, "There it is — seven!" Then she opened her coat and had nothing on underneath. She quickly picked up all the money on the table and took off.

Gaston looked at Boudreaux and asked, "Did she roll saven, sha?"

"How ahm posta kno, me?" asked Boudreaux. "Ah taut you wuz watchin' da dice!"

When You're Hot You're Hot

Boudreaux and Kymon decided to go to the casino. Once there, they thought it would be best to split up.

Boudreaux said, "Ahm gonna play rat here, and you go ova dere on da udda end o' da casino and play. "

After playing awhile and losing all his money, Kymon thought he'd go see if Boudreaux was having any luck. What he found was Boudreaux laughing and having a blast.

"Wat's da matta witchu, Kymon?" asked Boudreaux. "Ya look so sad!"

"Sha Lawd. Ah lost all my money, me," said a disappointed Kymon.

"May, you gotta find you a hot machine like me," said Boudreaux. "Watch dis. Arrytime ah put me a dolla bill in dis slot machine dere, ah win me four quarters!"

You Win Some And Lose Some

Boudreaux called Chlotilde to inform her that he had won the Lousiana Lottery.

"Hey beb," said Boudreaux excitedly, "ah jis found out, me, dat ah won da lottry. Hurry up and pack yo bags!"

"Dat's so sweet o' you, sha, ta take me on a vacation," said Chlotilde. "Should ah bring my winta clothes or my summa clothes?"

"You kin take dem all cuz ah jis wantchu outa da house, me!" explained Boudreaux.

Second Guessing

Turning to the best player of the Pedro foursome, the novice, Boudreaux asked, "How woodju have played dat last hand dat ah had, me?"

"Unda an assumed neem!" blurted Cowan.

Total Concentration

You just might be a Cajun if...

You have a pain in your shoulder and think you're having a problem with your rotating cup.

You're having difficulty getting pregnant and decide to try artificial insulation.

Your description of a gourmet dinner includes the words "Deep Fried Fat."

You describe a yard of boudin and cracklins as "breakfast."

You park your car under the car porch.

Chapter 6

Boudreaux On Health Care

The High Cost of Medicine

T-Boy's cat was hit unconscious by a car. He took him to Boudreaux since he was known to have the healing powers of a traiteur.

Boudreaux placed the cat on the kitchen table and looked very closely at it. He examined him from every angle and said, "Ah tink ah kin hep him, me."

He placed his hand, with palm down, about six inches above the cat and slowly began moving it across the entire length of its body. As he moved his hand he was making the sound, "hmmmmmmmmmmmm." Boudreaux came back to the original point and made the motion and sound again. Then he did it a third time. The cat woke up.

Boudreaux looked at T-Boy and said, "You kin take him home na. Ah tink he goin' be alrat, me. Jis give him dese two pill tonite wit his milk."

T-Boy said, "May, ah don't kno how ta tank you, Boudreaux. How much ah owe ya?"

Boudreaux answered, "Dat goin' be $310.00, sha."

"Sha Lawd, Boudreaux, dat's some expansive pills!" exclaimed T-Boy.

"Aw, non," said Boudreaux. "Da pills wuz only $10.00. But da teree cat scans coss $100.00 apiece, dem!"

Reach Out And Touch

Boudreaux's wife, Chlotilde, went to the doctor for her annual physical checkup. After a thorough examination, he said, "I have some good news and some bad news for you."

"Wat's da good news, doc?" asked Chlotilde.

"You're in perfect health and I can't find a thing wrong with you," said the doctor.

"Well wat's da bad news den?" questioned Chlotilde.

"You're pregnant!" replied the doctor.

Since Chlotilde was passed the normal child-bearing age, she rushed out of his office in a rage upon hearing this news. Getting home, she quickly telephoned Boudreaux at work.

"You ole goat, you, Boudreaux! Ya got me pregnant!" she screamed in the telephone.

After a long pause Boudreaux said, "May who's dis?"

Bundles Of Joy

Boudreaux, Shawee and Cowan were at the hospital. Their wives were expecting and about to deliver. They paced back and forth nervously. Suddenly the doctor came into the waiting room with the good news. He looked at Shawee and said, "Congratulations! You are the father of twins!"

"Huh, may dat make sanse yeah cuz, me, ah work fo' da Deuce Plumbing Company," said Shawee.

The doctor glanced at Cowan and said, "I know you'll be excited to know that your wife just had triplets."

"Sha Lawd. Dat don't surprise me, non, cuz ahm da manager o' da Teree M Company."

Boudreaux started to flee the waiting room as the doctor looked in his direction. "What's the matter with you? Where are you going?" asked the doctor.

"Ahm gitting outa here, me," exclaimed Boudreaux, "cuz me, dere, ah drive a delivery truck fo' da Saven-Up Cumpny!"

A Great Deal

Boudreaux was in the dentist office and asked, "How muchu charge fo' pulling an achin' toot?"

"Well, with gas, I charge $75.00," replied the dentist.

"Sha Lawd, dat's planny high, yeah," said Boudreaux. "But wat if ya take dat needle, poke it aroun' dat toot, put a lil novacaine in dere and den pull it?"

"Then that would be $50.00 an extraction," explained the dentist.

"Chooooo! Ah tink dat's still high, me!" exclaimed Boudreaux. "Den wat if ya take dem pliers, reach in and jis yank dat sucka outa dere?"

"Oh, I guess I could do that for five bucks," answered the dentist.

"Dat's mo' like it!" said a jubilant Boudreaux. "Hey, Chlotilde! Come git in da chair, beb. He goin' take you now!"

High Pain Tolerance

Boudreaux was doing some patchwork on the porch when he got a splinter stuck under his fingernail. It was deeply imbedded and he realized that he needed to see a doctor.

As Dr. Fontenot looked at it he said, "Boudreaux, that splinter is in there very deep! I'm going to have to stick a needle in your finger to deaden it so I can remove it."

"Don't worry bot dat, doc," said Boudreaux. "Jis go head and pull it out."

"But Boudreaux, it's going to hurt!" said Dr. Fontenot.

"Dat's okay, doc. Don't let dat bodda ya. Ah done already had me da two most worstest peens dere is in da world. Jis pull it out!" prompted Boudreaux.

"But Boudreaux, you just don't understand. It's going to hurt a lot," warned the doctor.

"Doc," said Boudreaux, "ah kin take it, me. Like ah said, ah done already had da two most worstest peens in da world so go head and pull it out!"

"Okay, but hold on," cautioned the doctor.

Boudreaux remained still, sweating buckshot, as Dr. Fontenot removed the splinter.

"Boudreaux, I would have never believed that one man could stand so much pain if I hadn't seen it with my own eyes," exclaimed Doctor Fontenot. "But I just have to know. What were the two pains you experienced worse than this."

"Well, doc," said Boudreaux, "ah wuz hunting duck in da marsh a few years ago wen here come some duck ovahead. So, me, ah squat down in da wata ta hide wen one o' dem nutria trap got me rat in da groin! Pooooo! Dat wuz da sacand worstest peen in da world."

"Wow!" cringed the doctor. "That must have hurt very much. But what could possibly hurt more than that?"

"Maaaaay, da most worstest peen wuz wen ah got ta da end o' dat doggone chain!" exclaimed Boudreaux.

Cajun To The Core

Cowan found out that Boudreaux was in the hospital and went to visit him. "Ah taut ya wuz on one o' dem safari hunting elephants in Africa, you," said Cowan. "Watchu doing here?"

"May, ah sho did go on dat elephant hunt, yeah, but dey hadta sand me home fo' an okeration wen ah got mysef hurt ova dere," replied Boudreaux.

"You got hurt by one of dem charging elephants?" asked a wide-eyed Cowan.

"Aw non, sha, nutting excitin' like dat. Ah got me dis hernia dere trying ta pick up one o' dem doggone decoy!" said Boudreaux.

Discerning Tastebuds

Boudreaux went into the hospital to have throat surgery. Each day as he is recuperating he drove the nurses crazy demanding his morning coffee. They checked with the doctor but he said no. They could only stand so much complaining so the head nurse went to the doctor again and pleaded to let Boudreaux have some coffee.

The doctor, also tired of Boudreaux's whining, said, "Okay, if he wants coffee that bad, he can have it. But since his throat isn't healed enough yet, he'll have to take it as an enema."

The nurse cheerfully returned to Boudreaux's room and told him what the doctor said. Needless to say, he wasn't completely thrilled with the news. Boudreaux reluctantly replied, "Ah really don't want dat but ah want my coffee bad bad, yeah. If dat's da only way ah kin have it, me, den go 'head."

As revenge for all those days of bellyaching, the nurse heats the coffee almost to the boiling point. She goes to Boudreaux's room and says, "Okay, Mr. Boudreaux, turn over." She inserts the tube and pours in the coffee.

"Yeoweeeeeeeeeeeeeee!" yelled Boudreaux.

"What's the matter? Too hot?" the nurse asks coyly.

"Aw non, beb. It's way too sweet!"

Caller I.D. Needed

Boudreaux excitedly called the doctor's office and shouted, "Doc, doc, ya gotta come quick. Chlotilde is in laba and da contractions is only two minute apart!"

"Is this her first child?" asked the doctor.

"May non, couyon! Dis is her husband!" answered Boudreaux

The Right Prescription

Grandpa Boudreaux went in for his annual physical check-up on his 92nd birthday. A few days later the doctor saw the elder Boudreaux walking down the street with a gorgeous young lady on his arm.

"Man, you're really doing great, aren't you, Grandpa Boudreaux," observed the doctor.

"May yeah, sha, but ahm jis doin' watchu told me ta do," replied Grandpa Boudreaux. "Getta hot mama and be cheerful!"

"Oh no! That's not what I said," responded a worried doctor. "I said you got a heart murmur! Be careful!"

New Math

Three old men, Boudreaux, Shawee and T-Brud were at the doctor's office for a memory test.

"Shawee, what is three times three?" asked Dr. Fontenot.

"Two hundred saventy-fo'," replied Shawee.

Dr. Fontenot turned to T-Brud and said, "It's your turn. What is three times three?"

"Chewsday," answered T-Brud.

Looking at Boudreaux the doctor said, "Okay, now it's your turn. What is three times three?"

"Nine," responds Boudreaux.

"That's great," said the doctor. How did you get that?"

"May dat's so simple, sha. Ah jis subtracted two hundred saventy-fo' from Chewsday, me!" said Boudreaux.

Sex On The Brain

One of Boudreaux's old uncles, Nonk Jules, went to the doctor.

"Ah wanchu ta lower my sax drive," said Nonk Jules.

"You mean your sex drive, don't you?" inquired the doctor.

"Maaaaay, dat's wat ah said, me, my sax drive!" emphasized the senior Boudreaux.

"But Mr. Boudreaux, you're 92 years old," said the doctor. "It's all in your head!"

"May ah kno dat, sha," said Nonk Jules. "Dat's how come ah wanchu ta lower it!"

Saving The Best For Last

Boudreaux wasn't feeling well so he went to his doctor for a checkup. After a thorough physical examination and tests, his doctor concluded that he had contracted a rare disease which was always swift and fatal. In fact, he told Boudreaux that he had only three days to live so he should try to make the most of them.

He went home and gave Chlotilde the bad news and, naturally, she was just as distraught as he was.

Boudreaux said, "Ah kno wat ahm goin' do, me. Dis furst day, dere, ahm goin' git all my frans ova ta da house and we goin' drink beer all day long. We goin' pass us a good time, yeah." And that's exactly what they did. T-Brud, Shawee,

Kymon, Cowan, Gaston and T-Boy met at Boudreaux's house, drank beer and told stories late into the night.

On the second day, Boudreaux was a little groggy but still decided to watch tapes of some of his favorite television programs — "The Dukes of Hazard", "The Honeymooners", "Cooking With Justin Wilson" and "The Six O'Clock News." He wanted to be sure he got all of the intellectual stuff in first.

As he awoke on the third and final day, Boudreaux detected an aroma coming from the kitchen. He sniffed a few times but couldn't determine what it was. So he jumped out of bed and headed to the kitchen to find out what was cooking.

"Wat's dat ah smell, me, Chlotilde?" asked Boudreaux.

"Maaaaay, dat's my famous seafood gumbo," answered Chlotilde. "Can'tchu tell, you?"

"Sha Lawd, dat sho smell good, yeah!" said Boudreaux. "Ah tink ahm goin' have me a big bowl full rat na."

"Haw non. Ya can't do dat, you," countered Chlotilde shaking her finger at him.

"May how come?" asked Boudreaux.

"Cuz ahm saving dis fo' da wake tamorra nite!" explained Chlotilde.

Soaking In Luxury

Boudreaux hit the lottery again and came into some extra cash. He decided to spend it on Chlotilde.

"Now dat we got us some money, sha, you kin have anyting yo lil hart desire," said Boudreaux. "Tell me, beb, watchu want? Anyting ya say dere, you got it!"

"Dis might sound a lil crazy but it's someting ah wanted, me, arry since ah wuz a lil girl," answered Chlotilde. "One time ah saw dis beautiful actress take a milk bat. Soaking in dat battub full o' milk made her skin so soft and so purty. Dat's wat ah want me, a good milk bat."

"Chooooo, beb! Dat's all?" asked a surprised Boudreaux. "Ahm goin' come outa dis smelling lika rose, me. Ahm goin' go call dat dairy rat na."

So Boudreaux called the dairy in Thibodaux to place his order. Asked the clerk, "Do you want the milk pasteurized, sir?"

"Aw non, sha!" said Boudreaux. "Jis up ta her behind in da tub goin' be okay!"

Hungry But Healthy

"Ya kno Shawee, me dere, ah been watching all dat healt stuff on da six o'clock news and done decided ta chenge my eatin' habits, me." said Boudreaux

"May, dat's good, Boudreaux. A man yo' age gotta start watching dat ya kno. Watchu eatin'?" inquired Shawee.

"Ah naver eat food wit dem additives or preservatives, me!" boasted Boudreaux. "And ah naver buy anyting dat's been sprayed or fed camical grain."

"Chooooo, dat's great!" marveled Shawee. "Tell me, how ya feel?"

"Hungry sha, hungry!" moaned Boudreaux.

Anatomy Of A Woman

Boudreaux was reading the newspaper, turned to Kymon and said, "Didja kno dat a woman got a YET?"

"Aw non," said Kymon, "Ah ain't naver heard o' dat, me. Dere ain't no way dat a woman got a YET."

"Ahm telling you - a-woman-got-a-YET!" insisted Boudreaux.

"May wat make you say someting so stoopid like dat, you? Why ya tink a woman got a YET?" asked Kymon.

"Cuz it say so rat here in da newspaper," replied Boudreaux. "Look, da headline on da front page say, "Woman Shot, Bullet In Her Yet!"

Cajun Cough Remedy

Cowan had been struggling with a very bad cold. He decided to get out of the house and visit Boudreaux to get his mind off it and maybe get a little relief.

"Wat's da matta witchu, Cowan?" asked Boudreaux. "Ya look like ya don't feel so hot, you."

"Haw non. Ah got me dis bad, bad cold," replied Cowan. "Man ah sneeze and ah cough all da time, me. Ah tink ahm goin' hafta go ta da dockta and git someting fo' it."

"You don't gotta do dat, non," said Boudreaux. "Ah kno zackly wat ta do fo' dat, me."

"Watchu talkin' abot?" inquired Cowan.

"Sha, jis take you a bottle o'milk o' magnesia, a box o' ex-lax and a can o' prune juice and mix dem all togedda real good. Den you drink it straight down."

"Dat's goin' cure my cold?" asked Cowan.

"Aw non," answered Boudreaux, "but it sho goin' make ya tink twice befo' you cough or you sneeze!"

The Common Cure

"Sha Lawd, ah been having me dis bad, bad haidache fo' a coupla days na," said Gaston. "Wat kin ah do fo' dis?"

"Well," said Boudreaux, "ah had me one o' dem las week, and Chlotilde took me inta da bedroom dere fo' tan minutes and it went away as fas as ah kin snap my finga."

Gaston reached for his coat and said, "Well, ah done tried arryting else. Ya tink Chlotilde's at home rat now, you?"

Policy Is Policy

T-Brud went to the doctor and was led into an examination room. The nurse told him to undress.

"But ah don't havta take off all my clothes. Ah jis want da doc ta look at my toe," explained T-Brud.

"Our policy is that everyone who comes in here must undress," replied the nurse.

"Dat don't make no sanse ta me," moaned T-Brud as he began to disrobe.

Boudreaux could hear this conversation from the next room. He stuck his head in the door and said, "Huh, dat's nutting, T-Brud. Ah jis came in, me, ta fix da talavision!"

You just might be a Cajun if...

Fred's Lounge in Mamou means more to you than the Grand Ole Opry.

You had fun at a party and told your friends that "you passed a good time."

None of your potential destinations are north of the old Mississippi River Bridge.

You stand up when they play "Jolie Blonde."

Chapter 7

Boudreaux At The Hubba Hubba

Unwanted Growth

Boudreaux walked into the Hubba Hubba with a large bullfrog on his head.

"Where in the world did you get that?" asked the bartender.

"Well, you probably won't believe this," the bullfrog replied, "but it started as a little wart on my behind!"

New Math

Boudreaux, T-Boy and Gaston stopped at the Hubba Hubba for a drink. The bartender asked, "Watchu goin' have, fellas?"

T-Boy said, " Ahm goin' have a BL, me."

"BL? Wat's dat?" asked the bartender.

"Maaaaay, dat's a Bud Light!" answered T-Boy.

"Me dere, ahm goin' have a CL," said Gaston.

"You mean a Coors Light?" questioned the bartender.

"You got dat rat, sha!" said Gaston.

"And you, Boudreaux. Watchu want, you?" continued the bartender.

"Ah know zackly wat ah want. Ah want me a fifteen." responded Boudreaux.

"A fifteen! Wat's dat? the bartender questioned.

"Man, ya don't kno nutting, you," said Boudreaux. "Dat's a saven and saven!"

The Cajun Equalizer

Boudreaux was having a cold one at the Hubba Hubba. A huge Texien walked up behind him and tapped him on the shoulder. When Boudreaux turned around, the Texien hit him, and he fell unconscious to the floor.

The Texien told the bartender, "When he wakes up, tell him that was Judo from Japan."

When Boudreaux regained consciousness, he continued drinking his beer at the bar. A little later the Texien came behind him and smacked him again.

"Tell him that was karate from Korea," said the Texien to the bartender.

Boudreaux eventually picked himself up and sat on his stool. A third time the Texien popped him causing him to fall to the floor in a stupor.

"When he comes to, tell him that was Tai Kwon Do from China," instructed the Texien to the bartender.

Boudreaux woke up, dusted himself off and staggered out of his favorite watering hole. Thirty minutes later he returned and searched out the Texien. Boudreaux walked up behind him and struck him with all of his might — pagowww!!!

Boudreaux looked at the bartender and said, "Wen he wake up dere, sha, tell him dat wuz crow bar from da Wal-Mark."

Celebrating Success

Boudreaux and Shawee were once again at their favorite watering hole, the Hubba Hubba. They ordered a beer and quickly drank it. Their eyes were filled with excitement, and they leaned over and gave each other a high-five.

As they did so, Boudreaux said, "Twanny-saven days! All riiiight!"

They ordered another round, engaged in a high-five and Boudreaux said with even more gusto, "Twanny-saven days! All riiiight!"

This went on for a few more rounds until the bartender became totally annoyed. Finally, in aggravation, he asked, "Look, you guys have been going through this ritual of ordering a drink, high-fiving and shouting 'all riiiight.' What in the world is going on?"

"May sha, we so prod, us!" said Boudreaux. "Me and

Shawee, dere, went ta da Wal-Mark and bought us one o' dem jigsaw puzzle ya kno. And on da outside da box it say, jis as pleen as day, teree ta six years. But lemme tellya, sha, me and Shawee done finished it in only twanny-saven days! We good, yeah!"

Dog Eat Dog

Boudreaux rushed into the Hubba Hubba and shouted, "Somebody got da numba fo' 911? We got us an emergency, us!"

"What's going on?" asked a Texien sitting at the bar.

"Is dat yo' truck wit da Great Dane in da back?" asked Boudreaux.

"That's right," said the Texien. "What's the problem?"

"Sha Lawd," said Boudreaux. "Ah got some bad news fo' you, yeah. My dog done killed yo' dog!"

"What kind of dog you got?" asked the stunned Texien.

"Me dere, ah got a lil Chihuahua," chimed Boudreaux.

"A Chihuahua!" yelled the Texien. "How in the world could that happen? Explain to me son how that tiny dog of yours can kill that great big animal of mine!"

"Well, ta tell da troot, podna, he got stuck in yo dog's troat and he choke ta deat," responded Boudreaux.

A Picture's Worth A Thousand Words

Boudreaux and Gaston were engaging in one of their favorite pasttimes at the Hubba Hubba. Everytime Boudreaux would drink a beer, he would pull something out of his pocket and sneak a glance at it.

Needless to say, this aroused Gaston's curiosity. "Oh, Boudreaux! How come arrytime ya finish a beer you look at someting in yo pocket, you? Watchu got in dere?" asked Gaston.

"Well, ta tell da troot, ah got me dis pitcher o' Chlotilde. And wen she start ta look good, dere, den ah kno dat ah done had enuff ta drink and it's time fo' me ta git home," explained Boudreaux.

On The Wagon

Boudreaux and T-Brud had just finished a work hitch offshore. Naturally they stopped at a local watering hole, the Hubba Hubba, for a few cold ones. After awhile, they each took one for the road and headed home. Looking in his rear view mirror, Boudreaux could see the flashing lights of a state trooper's car.

"Shaaaaa, we can't git caught wit dese beers, non!" said Boudreaux. "We gonna be in big trouble, us. Jis do like me, T-Brud."

Boudreaux chug-a-lugs his beer, peels the label off of the bottle of Budweiser, sticks it on his forehead and shoves the bottle under the seat. T-Brud does the same.

"You guys been drinking?" asked the trooper.

"Ah non, officer," said Boudreaux. "We don't drink no mo'. We on da patch, us!"

Family Reunion

A Texien walked into the Hubba Hubba and sat next to two locals. It was obvious they had been drinking for quite awhile. Seated where he was, he couldn't help but overhear their conversation.

"Ware you from, you?" asked the first one.

"Rat here in Galliano," replied the second local.

"May me, too!" said the first. "Ware you live?" he inquired.

"On tirty sacand street," answered the second.

"Chooooo, dat's someting, yeah! Me too!" said the first. "May wat house ya live in?"

"House number 289," responded the second.

"Caaaaaw, ah can't bleave dis. Me too!" said the first excitedly.

The Texien look at the bartender and asked, "Who are these guys?"

"Aw don't worry abot dem, sha," answered the bartender. "Dat's jis da Boudreaux twins drunk agin!"

Too Repetitious

Boudreaux was sitting by himself at the Hubba Hubba sipping a few cold ones. After awhile he turned to the guy seated next to him and asked, "May, sha. Ya wanna hear a good Polock joke, you?"

The guy showed his displeasure and replied, "I'd like you to know that I'm 265 pounds, a champion Golden Gloves boxer, and — I'm Polish."

He went on to say, "I'd also like you to know that the fellow next to me is 285 pounds of muscle and madness, a defensive lineman on a pro football team, and he, too, is Polish. Furthermore, the fellow seated next to him is just shy of 300 pounds, a professional wrestler and has the disposition of a hemorroidal pit bull. He's also Polish. Now, do you really think you want to tell that Polock joke in here, you dumb Cajun?"

"Sha Lawd, non!" responded Boudreaux. "Ah tink ah chenged my mind, me. Ah sho don't wanna havta 'spleen dat joke teree times!"

Economy Move

As Gaston picked up Boudreaux for one of their frequent visits to the Hubba Hubba, he noticed that Boudreaux was very subdued and had a sour expression on his face.

"Wats da matta witchu, Boudreaux? Ya look like ya been suckin' on some lemon, you," said Gaston.

"Ta tell da troot, last nite while ah wuz paying da bills, ah finely got fed up, me, wit da way dat Chlotilde trow money aroun'," answered Boudreaux. "So, me dere, ah storm in da living room and give her a great big lecture abot economy."

"Ya tink it done some good?" asked Gaston.

"Haw yeah, ah kno it done some good alrat!" exclaimed Boudreaux. "Taday we goin' sell my pirogue, my fishing gear and my shotgun!"

The Urine Test

Boudreaux walked into the Hubba Hubba and told the bartender, "Ah want me some tirty year old Scotch. Gimme a lil shot dere, podna."

The bartender figured that Boudreaux couldn't tell the difference between thirty year old scotch and any other, so he poured a shot of twenty year old stuff.

Boudreaux took a sip and spit it out.

"Dis ain't no tirty year old scotch, it's only twanny!" exclaimed Boudreaux. "Gimme wat ah axe ya fo' or ahm gonna go somewares else, me."

The bartender thought Boudreaux had just guessed right. He still didn't believe that he knew the difference, so he poured a shot of ten year old scotch and handed it to him.

Tasting it, Boudreaux once again spit it out and shouted, "Who you tink ya trying ta fool, you? Ahm gitting outa here, me!"

An elderly patron who had been sitting next to Boudreaux said, "Here ya go, son. Ah got watchu want. Go 'head and take a swig o' mine."

Boudreaux grabbed the glass and took a big sip. He quickly spit it out and had an awful look on his face.

"Caaaaaw, dat stuff taste jis like urine!" observed Boudreaux.

"Ya rat, yeah! Dat's zackly wat it is," said the wiley old gentleman. "Now tell me how old ah am, sha!"

Deep Thinker

Boudreaux and Shawee were engaged in one of their favorite activities at the Hubba Hubba. After guzzling down four or five brews, Boudreaux began to get philosophical.

"Ya kno, Shawee," said Boudreaux. "Dey got some tings, dere, dat don't make no sanse ta me, non."

"May like wat?" asked Shawee hesitantly.

"Maaaaay, dey say dat nutting kin stick ta teflon. Den how come dey kin make dat teflon stick ta da pan? Tell me dat!" challenged Boudreaux.

"Ah don't kno, me, and ah don't care!" said Shawee.

"Okay," said Boudreaux. "Ah got anudda one fo' ya. How come dey got some innastate highways dere in Hawaii? Sha Lawd, dat's confusing, yeah."

"Boudreaux, you tink too much, you. Jis drink yo beer!" said Shawee.

"Alrat well, 'spleen dis one ta me, den," continued Boudreaux. "How come dey put Braille dots on da keypad at da drive-up ATM? Huh? Tell me dat! Me dere, ah sho don't wanna be nowares aroun' if Stevie Wonder drive up, non!" exclaimed Boudreaux.

"Boudreaux, ya sho kin take da fun outa drinkin' beer, yeah!" said Shawee. "Behave yosef or ahm gonna call Chlotilde ta come pick you up! Ah got enuff o' dis, me."

"Okay, but wen ah fine out da ansa ta dese mysteries o' life ahm goin' tellya, yeah," warned Boudreaux. "Ah jis don't wanchu ta tink dat ahm jis anudda purty face, me!"

Full Of It

"You kno someting, Boudreaux," said T-Boy. "Some people got it and some people don't, but ta tellya da troot, you full o' it, you!"

Heavyweight

Boudreaux and Gaston were sitting at the bar at the Hubba Hubba. After consuming numerous bottles of their favorite beverage, Gaston asked, "Hey, Boudreaux. Wat's da difference between a wife and a girl fran?"

"Uuuuuh, bot forty-five pounds," answered Boudreaux as he raised the bottle to his lips.

69

Razor Sharp

While they were on the subject of girl friends, Gaston said to Boudreaux, "Ah decided, me, dat ahm gonna quit goin' out wit married wamans."

"May how come?" asked Boudreaux.

"Becuz o' my throat." answered Gaston.

"Cuz o' yo troat?" asked Boudreaux. "Wat dat got ta do wit it?"

"Cuz one o' dem husbands, dere, he taretened ta cut it!" replied Gaston.

Cajun Trailblazer

You just might be a Cajun if...

Directions to your house include "Turn off the paved road."

You refer to Louisiana winters as "Gumbo Weather."

You decide to "take" a walk.

You use a hose pipe to water the lawn.

Chapter 8

Boudreaux On Life

A Mouthful

Boudreaux and Chlotilde had just gotten into bed for the night when he told her, "Ah kno ah ain't goin' git me no sleep tonite, non. You goin' talk all nite long, you."

"May, wat make ya say dat, beb?" asked Chlotilde.

"Ah kin tell, yeah," said Boudreaux, "cuz you lef ya teet in!"

On The Wrong Track

Boudreaux and Gaston were walking and came upon a set of tracks. They extended as far as the eye could see.

"Man, dat's da most prettiest set o' deer tracks ah naver did see," said Gaston.

"Caaaaaw, you stoopid, yeah, you. Don'tchu kno nutting? Dat's a set o' rabbit tracks if ah aver did see some, me," replied Boudreaux.

They kept arguing back and forth — deer tracks, rabbit tracks, deer tracks, rabbit tracks, deer tracks, rabbit tracks — until finally a train came and ran over both of them.

What's In A Name

Boudreaux won $100,000 playing the Louisiana Lottery and decided to celebrate by going to New York to see the New Orleans Saints play the Jets. While there, he wanted to live the life of luxury, so he thought he would stay at the Waldorf Astoria Hotel.

Upon checking in, he told the clerk, "Ah want me da bess room you got in dis hotel, sha."

The clerk replied, "Sir, we have rooms that range in price from $200 to $2000 a day. What would you like?"

"Haaaaaw may, ah don't even gotta tink abot it. Gimme dat two tousand dolla room. Ahm goin' really treat mysef, me," said Boudreaux.

"Fine. Sign here," said the clerk.

Boudreaux took the pen and made an "x" on the registration book.

"Sir," said the clerk, "with that particular priced room comes certain amenities. For instance, you will have a female escort at all times. But it will be necessary for you to sign this other form in order to complete the paperwork.

Boudreaux picked up the pen again, looked at the form, and put an "o" where it called for his signature.

The clerk asked him, "Sir, why did you put an "o" for your name on this form and an "x" in the registration book?"

"Maaaaay, you don't tink ah want dat woman ta kno my real neem, me!" said Boudreaux.

Blackened Chicken

"Hey Boudreaux. Ah hear dat you burn some chicken, you. How dat happen?" asked T-Boy.

"Ah jis bake it a lil too long, me, dat's all," replied Boudreaux

"Watchu mean too long?" questioned T-Boy.

"May ah bake it for teree and a haf days," answered Boudreaux.

"How come you did someting stoopid like dat, you?" inquired T-Boy.

"Cuz it say rat dere on da recipe ta bake it a haf hour fo' array pound and ah weigh a hundred tirty pounds, me!" responded Boudreaux.

The Naked Truth

Boudreaux and Gaston were discussing some of their most embarrassing moments in life.

Said Boudreaux, "Pooooo! Ah kin remamber, me, my most worstest time."

"Aw yeah," said Gaston. "Wat wuz dat, sha?"

"Maaaaay, ah got me dis invitation in da mail ta one o' dem real fancy Mardi Gras Ball you kno, and it say pleen as day on dat invitation, 'Black Tie Only.' Talk abot embarrassed, me, wen ah git dere and see dat arrybody wuz wearing dere suits, too!" said Boudreaux.

You're In The Army Now

Boudreaux had a beautiful pair of sideburns when he was inducted into the Army. As he climbed into the chair, the barber asked, "Hey Boudreaux, wanna keep yo' sideburns?"

"Haaaaaw yeah!" answered Boudreaux with excitement.

"Catch!" said the barber.

Load Limit

Shawee came to visit Boudreaux who happened to be taking care of his fifteen month old nephew. The little fellow was walking around, and his diaper was hanging so low that it almost touched the floor.

Said Shawee, "Boudreaux, ya need ta chenge dat lil boy's diaper, yeah. It's so full o' pooh dat it's draggin' da flo'."

"Aw, non. It's not time, yet." replied Boudreaux. "Dey say rat here on da box dat it's good from fifteen ta twanny pound. He still got a lil mo' ta go!"

Cajun Standard Time

A Texien stopped at the local gas station. It was about 5:00 P.M. and the sun was already starting to set. He decided to strike up a conversation with Boudreaux who was at the next pump so he said, "I sure hate when daylight saving ends and we lose that hour, don't you partner?"

Boudreaux replied, "Ta tellya da troot, on da bayou here it stay light til it git dark, so it don't make no matta ta me."

Beauty Is In The Eye Of The Beholder

Boudreaux and Kymon were in San Francisco on vacation and stayed at a fancy hotel. While getting on the elevator, Boudreaux thought it wise to give Kymon some advice.

Said Boudreaux, "Kymon, ya gotta be vary careful 'round here, yeah, cuz dey got dem 'call girl' all ova da place."

"Aw, ah don't belief dat, non, me," replied Kymon.

"Ahm telling you, sha. Ya betta keep an eye out, yeah," said Boudreaux.

The elevator stopped on the fourth floor and a gorgeous woman got in.

Boudreaux leaned over and whispered in Kymon's ear, "Dat's one o' dem 'call girl' rat dere. Ah kin tell, me."

"Aw non. Dat can't be," responded Kymon, "She look so sweet and innocent, her."

"Watch me dere. Ahm goin' sho ya," said Boudreaux.

"Hey, sha. Wanna come ta my room wit me and pass a good time?" inquired Boudreaux.

"How much money are you offering, honey? asked the woman.

"Chooooo! Ah got me a tan dolla bill rat here," answered Boudreaux, waving the money in the air.

The woman was highly insulted and indignantly walked off the elevator on the fifteenth floor.

"Man, ah naver taught dat woman wuz like dat, non!" said Kymon. "She sho fool me. Tank ya fo' heping me out dere, Boudreaux."

"Jis be careful while you here, you. Be sho ya don't letchu gard fall down, non." cautioned Boudreaux.

The next morning Boudreaux and his wife, Chlotilde, were having breakfast in the hotel restaurant. Along comes the woman who was in the elevator with Boudreaux and Kymon the night before. As she passed by, she recognized Boudreaux and approached his table. She looked directly at him, pointed to Chlotilde and said with a smirk, "See what you get for $10.00!"

Wrong Number

Boudreaux and T-Brud were in deep conversation. T-Brud wanted to know the difference between the words "aggravation" and "irritation."

"Pass me dat talafoam book dere, " said Boudreaux. "Ahm goin' sho ya da difference rat now."

Boudreaux selected a number at random from the book, dialed it and a woman answered.

"Hallo," said Boudreaux. "Ahd like ta talk wit Boudreaux."

The woman replied sweetly, "I'm sorry, sir, but you have the wrong number."

Boudreaux apologized and hung up. He waited a minute and then redialed the woman's number. "Kin ah talk wit Boudreaux, please?" he said when the woman answered.

"You must be the same gentleman who called before," she said. "I'm sorry, but you've dialed the wrong number again."

He apologized once more. A minute later he dialed the same number and said, "Uuuuuh, lemme talk wit Boudreaux."

The woman by now was obviously angry. "Look, I've told you twice that there's no Boudreaux living here! Don't bother me again!" With that, she slammed the phone down.

Boudreaux turned to T-Brud and said, "Now, you see dere, T-Brud. Dat's irritation. Na ahm goin' sho ya wat aggravation is."

Boudreaux dialed the number again. When the woman answered, he said, "Oh beb, dis is Boudreaux. Annybody call fo' me?"

All In A Days Ride

Boudreaux telephoned his cousin in Texas and invited him to come visit his farm in Louisiana. He described his 40 acres of property he had along with an extra acre used for his garden. There he grew all kinds of vegetables.

A few days later his cousin showed up and after the appropriate chitchat, Boudreaux took him on a tour of his property. Twenty minutes later they reached the big canal in the back, and Boudreaux asked him what he thought of all that land.

His cousin, the Texien, said, "You know, partner, back in Texas when I ride on my property I leave at sun up and don't get to the end of it til sun down."

Boudreaux thought about that for awhile and said, "Ya kno, sha, ah usta have me a pickup truck jis like dat, too, yeah!"

Going For The Prize

Boudreaux was standing motionless in his sugar cane field. Kymon came by and noticed this right away and wondered what he was doing. Not knowing what to make of it, he just observed him for a few minutes. Nothing changed. Boudreaux just continued to stand still.

His curiosity got the better of him. So Kymon inquired, "Oh Boudreaux. How come you jis standing in da field like dat? Watchu doin', you?

"Maaaaay, ahm trying ta win dat Nobel Peace Prize, me," answered Boudreaux.

"Tell me how ya goin' do dat jis by standing aroun' da way ya doin'," challenged Kymon.

"Me dere, ahm doing zackly wat da people in charge told me ta do." said Boudreaux.

"Dey tolju ta do dis?" asked Kymon.

"Haw yeah," said Boudreaux. "Dey say fo' me ta have a chance ta win dat prize, dere, dat ah got ta be outstanding in my field!"

Not So Smart

Boudreaux was driving down the big road (I-10) in Houston. Suddenly this huge Texien cut him off and forced him onto the shoulder. Boudreaux immediately got out of his country Cadillac (pickup truck), walked up to the Texien and began screaming at him in a fit of anger.

The Texien remained calm, politely opened his trunk and pulled out a tire tool. He bent over and drew a circle on the ground. He then instructed Boudreaux to stand in it and not to get out under any circumstances!

Then the Texien walked over to Boudreaux's pickup truck and bashed in the tail lights. He looked over at Boudreaux and saw him bent over laughing.

Getting frustrated, the Texien bashed in the back glass. Looking over at Boudreaux again, he saw him lying on the ground, rolling from laughing so hard.

This really got the Texien upset, so he bashed in the front windshield, headlights and mirrors. Walking over to where Boudreaux was in the circle, he could see him laughing so hard that he wet his pants.

Not understanding why, the Texien said to Boudreaux, "Partner, I bash in your tail lights and you laugh. I bash in the back glass and you laugh even harder. Then I bash in your windshield, mirrors and headlights and you can barely breathe because you're laughing so hard. What in the world is wrong with you?"

Boudreaux said, "All yall Texiens tink yall so smart, yall. But ah got news fo' you. You ain't dat smart, non. Wen ya wuzn't lookin', me dere, ah got outta dat circle teree times!"

News From The Bayou

"Dear Junya,

Ahm writin' dis letta real slo cuz ah kno ya don't read too fas, you.

We don't live ware we did wen you lef. Yo mama read in da paper dat mos accidents happen witin twanny miles o' da home, so we taut it would be mo' safa fo' us ta move.

Ah ain't gonna be able ta sand ya da address cuz da las family dat lived here took da numbas off da house wit dem fo' dere next house, so dey wouldn't have ta chenge dere address.

It only rain twice dis week, teree days da furst time and fo' days da sacond.

Ya kno da coat ya wanted me ta sand ya? Well, Tante Weeza say dat it would be too havy ta sand wit dem great big button on it so we cut dem off and put dem in da pocket.

We got a letta from da funral home. Dey say if we don't make dat las payment on Grandma's funral bill, up she come.

Yo' sista had a lil T-bebe dis mornin'. Ah ain't heard wetta it's a boy or a girl, so ah dunno if you an aunt or an uncle. Ahm goin' letchu kno wen ah fine out, me.

Yo' nonk Joe fell in da whiskey vat yestiddy. Some o' dem men try hard ta pull him out but he fought dem off like crazy. He drowned so we end up cremating him. Pauvre bete, he burn fo' teree days, him.

Yestiddy, while yo' nonk Bill wuz shopping at Dillard's in Houma, da power went off. Shaaaaa, he stayed stuck on dat escalata fo' teree hours, him.

Some mo' bad news, sha. Teree o' yo' frans went off da bridge in a pickup truck. One wuz driving, da udda two wuz in da back. Da driver he got out, him. He roll down da winda and swam ta safety. But da udda two dey drowned. Dey jis couldn't git dat tailgate down.

Well, ah guess dat's all da news ah got fo' ya now. But wen someting else come up dere, ahm goin' wrat ta letchu kno, yeah. So be on da look out. Until ah see ya sumo.

Yo' luvin' poppa,
Boudreaux

Too Close For Comfort

Boudreaux was attempting to explain and rationalize his recent fender bender to Gaston. He said, "Pooooo, dey sho got some tarrible driver out dere on da road, yeah."

"May watchu mean?" asked Gaston.

"Caaaaaw, it jis aggravate me planny dat so manny o' dem people drive so close in da front o' me!" explained Boudreaux.

Rain, Rain Stay Away

T-Boy was complaining about getting a parking ticket from a meter maid in New Orleans.

"Pooooo! Ah don't naver git none of dem ticket, me!" bragged Boudreaux.

"How you do dat, you?" asked an amazed T-Boy.

"Maaaaay, ah jis take da windshield wipa off my caw befo' ah go dere!" explained Boudreaux.

Ungraceful Aging

Boudreaux was celebrating his birthday. As he was admiring himself in the mirror, he looked at Chlotilde and said proudly, "Ya kno beb, ah sho don't tink ah look 35 non, me. Watchu tink?"

"You rat yeah, sha, you don't," said Chlotilde. "Butchu usta!"

A Generous Victim

Boudreaux was walking in the French Quarters in New Orleans when he was attacked by two muggers. He fought back valiantly. Finally, after a furious battle, the felons subdued him. They went through his pockets and came up with a total of 57 cents.

"You mean to tell me," said one of the muggers, "that you fought that hard for a lousy 57 cents?"

"Caaaaaw, dat's all ya wanted, you?" asked Boudreaux. "May if ah wooda knowed dat, me, ah wooda give it ta ya. But me, dere, ah taut you wuz afta dat $500.00 ah got in my shoe."

A Great Deal

Shawee was running a used car lot, and Boudreaux stopped by to check it out. He saw a little Ford Mustang that he really liked and asked Shawee, "How mucha want fo' dat lil caw ova dere?"

"Six hundred dolla," said Shawee.

"Chooooo! Dat's kinda high, huh?" said Boudreaux.

"Yeah, butchu a good fran, you," said Shawee. "Tellya wat. Ah gonna give ya twanny pacent off."

"You'd take twanny pacent off fo' me?" asked Boudreaux.

"Haw yeah. Wait rat here cuz ah gotta go 'cross da street ta check someting out." said Shawee.

Shawee walked across the street to the cafe where his girl

friend was working and said, "Hey Maree, come see, beb.· Tell me dis. If ah give ya $600 and ah tellya ta take off twanny pacent, how much woodju take off?"

"Arryting but da shoes, sha!" said Maree.

New Image

Boudreaux was talking with his third cousin, Poo Poo Boudreaux, and noticed that he looked a little depressed.

"Lemme axe ya someting, Poo Poo," said Boudreaux. "You look kina down? Wat's da matta witchu, sha?"

"Ta tell da troot, it's my neem," replied Poo Poo. "People laff wen ah tell dem wat it is, and it make me feel bad bad, yeah. It really affect my sefless steam."

"Den wat kin ya do abot it?" asked Boudreaux.

"Ah wuz kina tinking 'bot gitting my neem chenged, me," said Poo Poo.

"Dat sound lika good idear, yeah, but wat woodja chenge it to?" inquired Boudreaux.

"Oooooh, ah dunno," answered Poo Poo. "Probly ta Poo Poo Guilbeau or someting like dat."

Economy Run

"Oh Boudreaux," said Cowan, "da udda day ah saw ya running behind da bus. How come ya wuz doin' dat?"

"May ah wuz jis tryin' ta save da quarta dat ah wooda had ta pay ta ride da bus," replied Boudreaux.

"Den why don'tcha try runnin' behind a taxi? Ya could save yosef a buck and a haf!" said Cowan laughing.

The Poor Old Days

Boudreaux and Kymon were reminiscing about how poor they were growing up.

Said Kymon, "We wuz so po' us wen ah wuz a lil boy dat da only ting ah had ta play wit wuz da ring aroun' da battub."

"Huh, dat's nutting!" exclaimed Boudreaux. "We wuz so po' dat by da time ah got my furst pare o' shoes dere, ah hadta put some gravel in dem ta git usta dem."

Boudreauxs Galore

"Caaaaaw, dey got sooooo manny Boudreaux's in Sot Loseiana," observed Gaston.

"May ah kno dat, me," said Boudreaux.

"In fac, dey got so manny dat dey say if ya trow a stick in da bushes dere, if a rabbit don't come runnin' out, a Boudreaux will!" laughed Gaston.

Out Of This World

"Didja hear on da six o'clock news las nite bot da restrunt on da moon?" asked Boudreaux.

"Sha Lawd, non!" said Cowan. "Ah din kno nutting abot dat, me. May wat dey say?"

"Dey say dat it got great food but don't got no atmosphere," laughed Boudreaux.

A Lot Of Bull

"Ya kno wat, Boudreaux," said T-Brud, "ah et meat all my life and ahm strong as a bull."

"Huh, dat don't cut no ice, non, " responded Boudreaux, "cuz ah et fish all my life, me, and ah still can't swam."

You just might be a Cajun if...

You have an "envie" for something instead of a craving.

You think gravy is a beverage.

You can look at a rice field and tell how much gravy it will take to cover the rice.

You say the gumbo was so good that you had two bowls.

Chapter 9

Boudreaux On Philosophy

A Deep Thought

Boudreaux and Gaston were vacationing in Hawaii and were on the beach soaking in some rays.

Boudreaux looked at Gaston and remarked, "Ya kno, Gaston, ah been tinking, me. Fo' Hawaii being one o' dem big tourist attraction dere, you sho don't see a whole lotta outa state license plate on dem caws, non."

This Bud's For Them

Boudreaux and Kymon were sitting at the kitchen table having a few beers. Each time Boudreaux opened the refrigerator, Kymon noticed something that appeared a little strange.

"Oh, Boudreaux," said Kymon, "Da top shelf, dere, in yo frige is fill wit beer, and ah kin undastand dat, me. But da bottom shelf is filled wit nutting but empty beer cans. How come ya keep all dem empty can o' beer in dere?"

"Maaaaay, dat's fo' all my frans dat don't drink!" explained Boudreaux.

Tuned In

Ole Boudreaux went to T-Boy's Barber Shop for a haircut. He was listening to a Walkman.

"T-Boy told him, "You goin' hafta take dem headphones off so ah kin trim around dem ears."

"Haaaaaw, non," replied Boudreaux. "Ah can't do dat, me. Ahm goin' die if ah do!"

T-Boy kept trying to trim around Boudreaux's ears but just couldn't get the job done. So finally, in frustration, he pulled the headphones off of Boudreaux's ears.

Sure enough, Boudreaux keeled over and fell to the floor unconscious.

T-Boy was shook up so he quickly picked up the headphones and put them on his ears to hear what was so important. As he listened he heard "breathe in-breathe out, breathe in-breathe out, breathe in-breathe out."

Can't Take It With You

Guilbeau was a wealthy old Cajun. As he was lying on his deathbed, he was trying to devise a plan that would allow him to take at least some of his considerable wealth with him.

He called for the three men he trusted most — his priest, his doctor and his good friend, Boudreaux. He told them, "Ahm goin' give ya each $30,000 in cash befo' ah die. At my funral, ah want yall ta place da money in my coffin so dat ah kin try ta take it wit me."

All three agreed to do this and were given the money. At the funeral, each approached the coffin in turn and placed an envelope inside.

While riding in the limosine to the cemetary, the priest said, "I have to confess something to you fellows. Ole Guilbeau was a good Catholic all his life, and I know he would have wanted me to do this. The church needed a new organ very badly so I took $10,000 of the money he gave me and bought one. I only put $20,000 in the coffin."

The doctor said, "Well, since we're confiding in one another, I might as well tell you that I didn't put the full $30,000 in the coffin, either. Guilbeau had a disease that could have been diagnosed sooner if I had had the latest in technology. But this machine cost $20,000 and I couldn't afford it then. I used $20,000 of the money to buy the machine so that I might be able to save another patient. I know that Guilbeau would have wanted me to do that, so I put only $10,000 in his coffin."

Boudreaux said, "Ah can't belief wat ahm hearing, me! Ahm so ashame o' bote o' yall. Wen ah put my anvelope in dat coffin, dere, it had my personal check fo' da full tirty tousand dolla!"

Any Excuse For A Party

Boudreaux was waiting nervously at his house because his wife, Chlotilde, was missing. He heard a knock at the door. It was his buddy, Cowan.

Said Cowan, "Boudreaux, ah got some good news and some bad news, me."

Boudreaux said sadly, "Den gimme da bad news furst."

"Ahm so sorry ta tell ya dis but we found Chlotilde drowned in da lake," answered Cowan.

"Sha Lawd! Poor Chlotilde! She wuz such a good woman, her!" said a visibly shaken Boudreaux. "May wat could be da good news?"

"Well, wen we pick her up outa da wata dere, she had teree dozen big blue crabs holding on. So gitchu some beer cuz we goin' have us a crab boil tonite!" explained Cowan.

Cajun Survival

Boudreaux began a fishing guide service and one day had a Mexican, Japanese and Englishman on the boat. They started to take on water and were sinking fast. Much to their dismay, there was only one life jacket on board.

Understanding the situation, the Mexican volunteered to jump overboard. He yelled "Viva Mexico!" and jumped in.

The Japanese, likewise, decided to make the sacrifice and yelled "Banzi!" as he made the leap into the lonely waters.

Then Boudreaux yelled "Iiiiiieeeeeee - Long Live The Cajuns!", grabbed the Englishman, and threw him overboard.

A Way With Words

Chlotilde went down to the local newspaper office and said she wanted to put in the obituary column that Boudreaux died.

They informed her that it would cost $1.00 per word and asked what she would like to have printed.

After some consideration she said, "Here's $2.00. Put in dere dat "Boudreaux Died.""

"Surely you must want more than that, Chlotilde," said the editor. "After all, you and Boudreaux have been married for such a long time."

"May non, beb," said Chlotilde, "jis put 'Boudreaux Died.' Dat be okay."

The editor continued, "Look, Chlotilde. You're just a little upset. Go home and give it some thought. Come back tomorrow and let us know what you've decided."

Chlotilde returned the next day and said, "You wuz rat, yeah! Ah do want someting else, me. Ah wanchu ta put in dere, "Boat For Sale.""

Taking The Edge Off

After a Saints football game, Boudreaux and Cowan wanted to treat themselves while in New Orleans. They decided to eat at a fancy restaurant, one in which you have to go inside and sit down. The waiter brought the menus and they proceeded to check it over.

Boudreaux asked, "Cowan, don't dis menu feel kina funny ta ya?"

"Huh, now datchu mention it, it sho do, yeah," replied Cowan.

When the waiter returned to take their order, they inquired about it. The waiter said, "You're absolutely right. It is a little different. You see, it's written in Braille so that blind people can read it."

"Chooooo, as fancy as dis menu is, sha, ah wouldn't take no chance on ruining it, me. You could spill some red bean or gumbo or someting on it. Me dere, ahd git dis ting laminated!" said Boudreaux.

The Name Game

Boudreaux and Shawee were sipping a cold one when Boudreaux looked at Shawee and said, "Shawee, lemme axe ya someting."

"May, go 'head," said Shawee.

"Wat do John da Baptist, Attila da Hun and Winnie da Pooh all got in common, dem?" asked Boudreaux.

After careful thought Shawee answered, "Ah don't kno, me. Wat?"

"Couyon, dey all got da seem middle neem!" laughed Boudreaux.

What's Good For The Goose

Boudreaux had just stumped Shawee on a riddle. Not to be outdone Shawee said, "Aw yeah, you tink ya so smart, you. Den go 'head and ansa dis one, big shot!"

"Take yo' bess shot," quipped Boudreaux, "Ahm ready, me."

Shawee said, "Arnold Schwarzenegger gotta long one, Brad Pitt, he gotta short one, Madonna, her, she don't even have one, and da Pope, he got one but he don't naver use it. Tink ya kno da ansa, smarty pants?"

"Huh, someting come ta mind rat away, but ah don't tink dat kin be rat," said Boudreaux. "Ah ain't goin' make no fool o' mysef, me, by saying dat, so go 'head and tell me."

"Maaaaay, a last neem!" answered a gloating Shawee.

Timely Research

Boudreaux was on a flight from Paris back to Cajun country. A tall, slender, gorgeous blonde woman was in the seat next to him. He wanted to strike up a conversation with her, but didn't quite know how. When the blonde pulled out a lap top and started working, he seized the opportunity.

"Watchu workin' on dere, sha?" asked Boudreaux.

"It's reseach data obtained through a comprehensive study to determine what kind of man a woman is most attracted to," answered the beautiful blonde.

"Chooooo! Dat's intresting," said Boudreaux. "Watchu fine out?"

"Well," said the blonde, "our study indicates that the type of man women are most attracted to are doctors. They're intelligent, professional, save lives and do a lot of good for mankind."

"Huh, dat make a lota sanse ta me, yeah," said Boudreaux.

"The next group," said the blonde, "is the Native American Indian. The study reveals that women are attracted to the richness of their skin, their dark hair and beautiful eyes. They are a very attractive people."

"Me dere, ah kin see dat, yeah," said Boudreaux. "May, who's da tird group, beb?"

"Oddly enough," said the blonde, "It's the Cajuns."

Boudreaux's heart started pounding so hard that he thought it would pop out of his chest. He excitedly blurted out, "May why, sha?"

"Because," answered the blonde, "they are fun-loving and have such a unique and interesting culture and language. By the way, we haven't been formally introduced. My name is Mary Smith. What's yours?"

"Maaaaay, Dr. Tonto Boudreaux!" responded ole Boudreaux.

Total Concentration

Cowan walked into Boudreaux's kitchen and found him staring intensely at a frozen can of orange juice.

"Wat in da world ya doing, you?" asked Cowan.

"Maaaaay, ahm jis following da directions, me. It say rat here on da package — 'concentrate'," said Boudreaux.

Courteous Driver

Boudreaux met up with Kymon on a bridge too narrow for two cars to pass.

"Hey Couyon," shouted Boudreaux, "ya goin' hafta back up, yeah, cuz me dere, ah don't naver back up fo' no idiot!"

"Don't worry bot dat, sha." shouted Kymon as he shifted in reverse. "Ah all da time do, me!"

A Hole In One

A few weeks after Boudreaux and Chlotilde were married, Boudreaux came home from work and found his bride upset and in tears.

"Wat's da matta, sha?" asked Boudreaux.

"Ah feel so tarrible, me," answered Chlotilde. "Ah wuz pressing yo suit, dere, and ah burn a great, big hole in da seat o' yo pants."

"Dat's all, beb?" inquired Boudreaux. "Den don't worry abot nutting. Remamber dat ah got me dat extra pare o' pants when ah got da suit?

"Aw, yeah," said Chlotilde.

"Den jis use dat ta patch up da hole!" explained Boudreaux.

Chef Boy-R-Boudreaux

Boudreaux was anxious to help his new bride in the kitchen, so Chlotilde gave him the task of slicing the onions. After a minute or so, his eyes began to water very badly.

Trying to be helpful, Chlotilde said, "Ya kno, beb, yo eyes wouldn't wata so bad, non, if ya cut dem onions unda wata."

"Maaaaay, if ah do dat, how ahm goin' breade, me?" questioned Boudreaux.

Nobody's Fool

Once when Boudreaux and Kymon were little boys, they were playing with a flashlight. Kymon turned on the beam, aimed it at the ceiling and said to Boudreaux," Ah dare ya ta climb ta da top, sha."

Boudreaux looked at him and said, "Haaaaaw, non. Ya must tink ahm stoopid or someting, you. Rat wen ah git ta da top, dere, you goin' turn it off!"

Don't Know Much About History

Boudreaux was at a Mardi Gras ball and was introduced to a psychiatrist.

"Hey doc," said Boudreaux, "Ah undastand, me, dat ya kin tell wetta or not a person dere is smart or not by axing some varry simple questions. Is dat a fac?"

"Yes, a very simple question," the doctor replied. "For example, Captain Cook made three voyages around the world and died on one of them. Which one?"

"Aw, Doc," said Boudreaux. "Dat's not fare. You kno ahm not no good in histry, me!"

Two Can Play The Game

Boudreaux was piloting a tug boat in New York Harbor. He passed by this huge ship that had HMS on its side. Boudreaux yelled at the ship's officer, "May wat's dat HMS on dat boat dere?"

The officer replied, "That stands for His Majesty's Ship."

"Aw, okay," said Boudreaux.

The next day Boudreaux pulls up next to the same big ship with his boat. On his boat he has DMB."

The officer said, "Hey Boudreaux. I see you came back."

"Haw yeah," said Boudreaux," and look wat ah got on da side o' my boat, me! Ya see dat?"

"Yes," said the officer. "But I have to admit that I've never seen anything like that before. What's that DMB?"

"Dat me boat!" said Boudreaux proudly.

Greatest Invention Ever

Boudreaux, Gaston and T-Brud were driving to work and engaged in conversation. They began discussing change and inventions that brought it about.

"Watchall tink is da most bestest invantion dat dere aver wuz?" asked Boudreaux.

"Me dere, ah tink it wuz da wheel," answered Gaston. "Cuz dat led da way fo' caws, treens and all udda kina ways ta git from one place ta anudda."

"Da wheel wuz good alrat, but, me, ah tink it wuz da talafoam," said T-Brud. "Da foam lettus talk wit people all ova da world and stay in touch wit dem. It made da world mo' smaller."

"And you, Boudreaux. Watchu tink, you?" asked Gaston.

"Maaaaay, dere's no doubt in my mind, sha, dat da most bestest invantion aver wuz da termos," responded Boudreaux.

"Da termos!" asked a shocked T-Brud. "How kinya say dat?"

"May dat's easy," answered Boudreaux. "Wen ah go ta work in da summa dere, Chlotilde, she fill my termos bottle up wit ice cold lemonade. And it stay cold cold all day. Den in da winta time, she fill up dat seem termos wit some hot cocoa and it stay hot hot hot all day long. How it kno dat?"

No Big Mystery

"Hey Boudreaux," said Shawee, "how come dey got so manny Boudreaux's in da talafoam book?"

"Maaaaay, cuz dey all got talafoams, dem!" replied Boudreaux.

ESP

Boudreaux and T-Brud were watching T.V. A commercial about a new movie came on, and at its conclusion said, "Coming to a theatre near you!"

Boudreaux looked at T-Brud and said, "Dat's someting, yeah! Ah wonda how dey kno ware we live, us?"

Put The Pedal To The Metal

Boudreaux was quite irritated as he talked with his teenage son, Junya.

"Junya!" said Boudreaux. "Ya mean ta tell me dat da skool is only teree block away and ya want ta drive dere? May watchu tink dem two feets ya got is fo', boy?"

"Maaaaay, one fo' da brake and da udda one fo' da gas!" explained Junya.

You just might be a Cajun if...

You think the head of the United Nations is Boudreaux Boudreaux Guillory.

You think the Mason-Dixon line is at Bunkie.

You consider Breaux Bridge the capital of the state and Lafayette the capital of the nation.

You pass up a trip abroad to go to the Crawfish Festival in Breaux Bridge.

Chapter 10

Boudreaux On Politics & The Law

The Wrong Question

Boudreaux was driving on a side street in New Orleans and went right through the intersection without stopping for a stop sign. A policeman saw this, pursued him and pulled him over.

"Didn't you see that stop sign? What's the matter with you, can't you read?" asked the cop.

"Haaaaaw, yeah," said Boudreaux, "but ah don't belief arryting ah read, me!"

None For The Road

A police officer pulled over Boudreaux who had been weaving in and out of traffic. He walked up to his car and said, "Sir, I need you to blow into this breathalyzer tube."

"Ahm sorry, officer, but ah can't do dat. Cuz me dere, ahm an asthmatic. If ah try ta do dat, ahm goin' have me a bad bad asthma attack."

"Okay, then I'll need you to come down to the station to give a blood sample," said the officer.

"Yabbut, ah can't do dat nedda, me," answered Boudreaux. "Ya see, ahm a hemopheliac and wit anny kind o' break in da skin ah could bleed ta deat."

"Well then, we'll need a urine sample," said the exasperated policeman.

"Ahm sho sorry but dat's outa da question, too," replied Boudreaux. "You see, me dere, ahm a diabetic and if ah do dat ahm goin' git really low blood sugar."

"Alright then, I'll need you to come out here and walk this white line," countered the impatient officer.

"Ah can't do dat nedda," said Boudreaux.

"Why not?" asked the officer.

"Maaaaay, cuz ahm drunk, me!" responded Boudreaux.

A Smelly Comparison

Boudreaux and Shawee were sitting at the bar at the Hubba Hubba getting "chockayed."

Shawee asked, "May Boudreaux, watchu tink abot dem term limit fo' politicians, you?"

"Maaaaay, ahm all in fava o' dat, me," answered Boudreaux.

"How come?" asked Shawee.

"Ya see me dere," said Boudreaux, " Ah tink dem politician ought ta be chenged on a reglar basis, jis like a lil baby's diaper — and fo' da seem reason!"

It's Not Who You Know

Boudreaux was working as a cop and while on patrol, stopped a motorist. He asked for his driver's license.

After careful examination, Boudreaux said, "Sha, ahm goin' hafta give ya two ticket. One o' dem fo' speeding and da udda one fo' not waring yo' eyeglasses. Yo' license sho dat dere's a restriction and ya gotta ware yo' glasses."

"Well," said the motorist, "I want you to know that I have contacts."

"Ah don't care who ya kno, me," said Boudreaux. "Ya goin' git dese ticket annyhow!"

No Legal Eagle

In an enlightening conversation at the Hubba Hubba, Gaston asked Boudreaux, "Hey, Boudreaux, tell da troot. Watchu tink abot Roe versus Wade?"

"May, dat's no big deal, non," said Boudreaux. "It all depand how deep da bayou is!"

At Your Service

Boudreaux was working at the law firm of Boudreaux, Boudreaux and Boudreaux. The telephone rang and Boudreaux answered. The caller asked for Mr. Boudreaux.

Boudreaux responded, "Ahm so sorry, me, but Mr. Boudreaux's in da courtroom."

The caller again asked for Mr. Boudreaux.

"May, Mr. Boudreaux's on vacation," answered Boudreaux.

The caller asked for Mr. Boudreaux a third time.

Boudreaux replied, "Maaaaay, speaking, sha!"

Not So Hot

Boudreaux, a lawyer, defended his client accused of murder. The jury returned a guilty verdict and sentenced him to the electric chair. As he was serving his time, Boudreaux appealed the case. He drove to the prison to give his client the news of the appeal.

"Ah gotchu some good news and some bad news, sha," said Boudreaux. "Da bad news is dat ya still goin' git da 'lectric chair."

"That's terrible!" said his stunned client. "What could possibly be the good news?"

"Maaaaay, ah gotchu da voltage lowered, me!" said Boudreaux proudly.

Shedding Light

Boudreaux ran for a seat on the Parish Council and won in a close race. At the first Council meeting, there was only a 60-watt bulb providing light for the group. Some of the Council members complained that there wasn't enough light to even read the agenda.

A motion was made and seconded to buy a chandelier for the Council chambers. During the discussion of the motion, Boudreaux said, "Ah can't see, me, how come yall wanta spand $46.88 fo' someting ta put in da meeting room wen it's so dark in dere alreddy dat ya can't see a doggone ting anyhow!"

Dead Right

Boudreaux was called as a witness in a murder trial. In his testimony he stated that he saw the victim lying on the ground, obviously dead. The defense lawyer rose to his feet and strenuously objected to the statement.

"Mr. Boudreaux, are you a doctor?" asked the lawyer.

"Haw non, not me," replied Boudreaux.

"Well then, are you a paramedic?" questioned the lawyer.

"Pooooo, ah guess not!" responded Boudreaux.

"Have you ever gone to medical school?" continued the lawyer.

"Sha Lawd, non," said Boudreaux.

"Then tell me, sir, how do you know the victim was dead?" pressured the lawyer.

"Cuz me dere, ah went ta da funral!" said a confident Boudreaux.

Louisiana Politics

Boudreaux worked hard for his candidate in the Justice of the Peace election. He was very surprised to find himself later brought into court.

"May, how come ya arrest me?" inquired Boudreaux.

"You are charged with voting seven times," the judge said sternly.

"Charged!" exclaimed Boudreaux. "Ah taut ah wuz gettin' paid, me!"

Sobriety Test

A state trooper stopped a speeding vehicle and began questioning the driver. He noticed some extremely large knives on the front seat and wanted to know why he had them in his possession.

"I'm a juggler with the circus and those are machetes I use in my act," explained the driver. "I was speeding because I'm late for my performance."

"If that's the case," said the trooper, "get out here and prove it to me."

The driver stepped out of his car and began juggling the

machetes. Boudreaux and Cowan happened to be passing at the time and witnessed this exhibition.

"Chooooo! Looka dat!" said Boudreaux. "Ahm goin' hafta watch da drinkin' and da drivin' cuz dat sobriety tess sho done got tuff!"

On The Wagon

Boudreaux walked into the Hubba Hubba and told the bartender, "Give me teree shots o' whiskey, one fo' bote o' my bess frans and one fo'me." Every day for the next week, he went into the bar and ordered the same thing.

The following week he went in and ordered two shots. The bartender looked disturbed and asked, "Boudreaux, wat happened? Did one o' yo' friends pass away?"

"Aw non, sha! Nutting drastic like dat. Ah jis quit drinkin' fo' Lent, me!" explained Boudreaux.

Ignorance Is Bliss

An election pollster was at the general store interviewing incoming customers. As Boudreaux entered the store, he was asked by the gentleman, "Excuse me, sir. I am conducting a poll. Would you say that you were uninformed or apathetic?"

Responded Boudreaux, "Ah don't git involve in dem politic. All ahm goin' told ya is dis: ah dunno me and ah don't care!"

Sign Of The Times

A state trooper stopped Boudreaux doing 62 in a 35-mile zone.

"May wat's da matta, sha?" asked Boudreaux.

"You were speeding, sir," said the trooper.

"May, dat can't be," said Boudreaux. "Ah wuz jis following da signs ah saw dat said '62.'"

"Those are highway route markers, not speed limits," informed the trooper.

"Sha Lawd, den good ting ya din see me back dere on Highway 95!" said Boudreaux.

Duty Calls

Boudreaux was summoned as a prospective juror. In questioning him, the judge asked, "Is there any reason you could not serve as a juror in this case, Mr. Boudreaux?"

"Ah jis don't wanna be away from my job dat long," answered Boudreaux.

The judge asked, "Can't they do without you at work?"

"Haw yeah!" exclaimed Boudreaux. "But ah sho don't want dem ta kno dat!"

An Unlikely Comparison

"Hey T-Brud," said Boudreaux. "Tell me someting, sha. How you tink boudin and a law is alike, dem?"

"Ah don't kno, me," replied T-Brud after careful reflection.

"You don't wanna kno how edda one is made!" laughed Boudreaux.

Backward And Forward

"Ah got one fo' you, sha." said T-Brud. "Wat's da oppazit o' progress?"

"Congress?" replied Boudreaux.

Nothing But The Truth

Boudreaux was a witness for the prosecution and had given damaging testimony against the defense which would adversely affect their case. The defense wanted to get back at him.

"Mr. Boudreaux, you seem to have more than the average share of intelligence for a man of your background and limited education," sneered the lawyer as he began his cross-examination.

"Sha, if ah wouldn't be unda oat dere, ahd return da compliment, yeah!" replied Boudreaux.

An Oxymoron

Boudreaux and Shawee were taking a shortcut home through the cemetary one night from the Hubba Hubba.

"Do dey aver bury two people in da seem grave?" asked Boudreaux.

"May non!" said Shawee. "How come ya axe someting stoopid like dat, you?"

"Cuz it say rat dere on da haidstone," answered Boudreaux, "here lies a lawya and an honest man!"

Cajun Generosity

Boudreaux and Cowan were walking by One Shell Square tower in New Orleans when the police caught two suspected felons in front of the building. The cops got out of the patrol car and ordered the two men to put their hands over their head against the building and spread their legs apart. They then went back to the car to radio for help.

Boudreaux and Cowan saw the two guys against the building, ran over quickly and asked, "Which way she falling boys? We wanna hep ya!"

You just might be a Cajun if...

You greet your long lost friend at the Lafayette International Airport with iiiiiieeeeeeeeeeee!

You don't know the real names of your friends, only their nicknames.

You get a disapproving look from your wife and describe it as, "She passed me a pair of eyes."

Someone touches you on the rear end and you say that, "He passed me the hand."

Chapter 11

Boudreaux On Relationships

The Morning After

Boudreaux came home from work one day and found Chlotilde crying.

"Wat's da matta, beb?" asked Boudreaux.

"Ah jis come from da dockta, me, and he say dat ah got less den twelve hour ta live!" explained Chlotilde. "We gotta make da mos o' da lil time we got lef so ah made us a big pot o' seafood gumbo. We goin' eat dat gumbo, drink us some wine and be romantic all nite long."

"Whoop! Hol on a minute dere, sha," cautioned Boudreaux. "Aw yeah, dat's fine fo' you. But me dere, ah gotta git up in da morning!"

The Right Partners

"Hey, Boudreaux," said Gaston. "Ah hear yo' ole Tant Flo wuz married fo' times, her."

"Dat's rat," answered Boudreaux. "She wuz married ta a banka, an acta, a minista and an undataka."

"Chooooo, dat sound lika strange combination ta me, yeah," said Gaston.

"Aw non," said Boudreaux. "It make good sanse wen ya stop ta tink abot it."

"How come you say dat?" asked Gaston.

"Maaaaay, it wuz one fo' da money, two fo' da sho, teree ta git ready and fo' ta go!" laughed Boudreaux.

Delayed Reaction

Boudreaux and his wife, Chlotilde, were sitting on their front porch swing without saying a word. All was quiet.

Then suddenly, without warning, Boudreaux backhanded her — "Pagowww!"

Startled, she asked, "May, watchu do dat fo', beb?"

Boudreaux answered, "Dat's fo' tirty years o' bad sex!"

They continued sitting in silence. A few minutes later Chlotilde retaliated. She smacked him with all her might across the head — "kaboooom!"

Boudreaux, rubbing his head asked, "Pooyie, how come ya did dat, you?

Chlotilde pointed her finger at him and shouted, "Dat's fo' knowing da difference!"

Forgotten Passion

Boudreaux and his three old uncles were sitting on a bench at Audubon Park. Three beautiful, shapely young ladies passed by and, needless to say, did not go unnoticed.

Nonk Jeaux, the 70 year old, looked at them and said, "Sha, Lawd. If ah wuz 50 years younger, ahd grab me one o' dem gals and give her a great big hug."

Nonk Nooch, the 80 year old remarked, "Ahd go mo' furter den dat, me. If ah wuz 50 years younger, ahd grab me one o' dem wamans and give her a tight hug and a big, big kiss — rat on da lip!"

The eldest of the three, 90 year old Nonk Pouchee, looked wide-eyed and said excitedly, "Me dere, if ah wuz 50 years younger, ah would grab me one o' dem chicks and give her a tight hug and a big, fat kiss and, and, and, and —- uhhh, Boudreaux, wat else ahd wanna do, me?"

Total Commitment

Boudreaux, a New Yorker and a Texien were trying to get into the CIA. All were successful in passing the preliminary tests, and it came down to the final one.

The instructor said, "This last test will give us an indication of your desire to be a member of the CIA. You must pass it in order to work for us." He looked at the guy from New York and said, "Your wife is in the next room. Here is a .38 revolver. Go in there and kill her."

The New Yorker was shocked and without hesitation said, "My wife is the mother of my four children and I love her very much. I wouldn't harm her in any way for anybody. I quit."

The instructor glanced at the Texien and told him, "Sir, your wife is in the next room. Take this .38, go in there and kill her."

The Texien responded, "She was my childhood sweetheart. I've loved her since I was ten years old, and she has been the only love in my life. I wouldn't hurt her for you or the CIA. Forget it. I'm getting out of here!"

The instructor looked at Boudreaux and gave him the same instructions as the other two. Boudreaux grabbed the gun, walked into the next room and then — bang, bang, bang, bang, bang, bang was heard. This was followed by a lot of kicking, screaming and hollering.

A bloodied Boudreaux opened the door, walked toward the instructor and said, "May, sha. How come ya din tell me dat dere wuz blanks in dat gun? I had ta end up strangling her, me!"

Big Winner

Boudreaux bought a service station and was trying desperately to promote business. In an effort to draw customers, he put up a sign saying, "Free sex with fillup."

Cowan came by and saw the sign. He asked, "Hey, Boudreaux. Wat's dis free sex wit a fillup all abot?"

Boudreaux replied, "Well, ya see, dat's jis da way it is. If ya git yo caw filled up, you git free sax."

"Sha Lawd! Ah could go fo dat, yeah, me!" said Cowan. "Go 'head and fill up my caw."

Boudreaux filled the tank and put the nozzle back on the pump.

"Now ware's da free sex?" asked Cowan.

"Non, non, non, ya gotta draw fo' it," said Boudreaux.

Boudreaux goes inside and comes out with a box full of numbers. Cowan reaches in and pulls one out.

"Wat numba didja git?" asked Boudreaux.

"Ah got me numba five," said Cowan.

"Aw non," said Boudreaux. "The winning numba is saven. Ahm sho sorry, sha, butchu lose."

The next week Cowan comes back and asks, "Ya still got dat ting wit da free sax, you?"

"Aaaaaw yeah!" said Boudreaux. So Cowan fills up his car again and draws a number from the box.

"Chooooo! Ah got me numba saven dis time. Now I win, me!" shouted Cowan excitedly.

"Aw non," said Boudreaux. "Dis week numba eight is da winna."

"Dis ting is a farce ahm tellin' ya!" shouted Cowan disgustedly. "It's a farce!"

"Haw non, it's not a farce and ah kin prove it ta ya, sha," said Boudreaux. "Cuz yo wife done won twice dis week already!"

Lost Cause

Boudreaux and T-Brud were sitting at the kitchen table drinking a cup of Community coffee.

Asked T-Brud, "Oh Boudreaux. Now datchu gitting up in age dere, how's da memory?"

"Jis as good as aver, knock on wood," answered Boudreaux as he rapped his knuckles on the table.

Two minutes later Boudreaux asked, "Somebody goin' git da door or wat?"

Fast Money

Boudreaux took out a million dollar life insurance policy on himself. T-boy was with him at the time.

"Boudreaux," asked T-Boy, "how long ya tink it goin' take Clothilde ta spand all dat money wen ya gone?"

"Haaaaaw. Ah don't kno, me. It jis depand on wetta or not she come ta da funral, her!" said Boudreaux.

All In The Family

Gaston stopped by Boudreaux's house early one morning and found him crying uncontrollably at the kitchen table.

"Wat's da matta witchu?" asked a concerned Gaston.

"Ah jis got some bad news, me — my poppa died," explained Boudreaux. Gaston did his best to console him and then left to take care of some errands.

Later that day Gaston dropped in again to check on his good friend. Much to his surprise, he found Boudreaux still in the kitchen "crying up a storm."

"Look, ah kno ya suffered a big loss losing yo poppa like dat and all, but how come ya still crying?" asked Gaston.

"Sha Lawd, it git mo' worser, yeah," said Boudreaux. "Ah jis called my brudda, dere, and his poppa died, too!"

More Than You Want To Know

Boudreaux and Chlotilde were in deep thought as they sat on the front porch swing.

Chlotilde asked, "Boudreaux, if ah die befo' you do, woodja remarry?"

"Sha Lawd, ahm so use ta living wit somebody, me, dat ah don't tink ah could live by mysef, non," said Boudreaux. "Ta be honest, beb, ah tink ah would hafta say yeah."

"Well, woodja bring her ta live in my house?" questioned Chlotilde.

"You kno dat dis is my house, too. And me dere, ah wouldn't wanna live nowares else. Haw yeah, ahd bring her here, Chlotilde," answered Boudreaux.

"Well den, woodja let her drive my new caw? asked a frustrated Chlotilde.

"Only if ah hadta, beb, like if she wuz going grocery shopping or someting. But ah wouldn't jis let her take it for a ride or nutting like dat, ya kno," responded Boudreaux.

"Boudreaux," asked Chlotilde, "woodja let her use my gulf clubs?"

Boudreaux thought for a while and then replied, " Ah non, sha. It wouldn't do her no good cuz she's lef handed, her!"

Cajun Feud

Boudreaux lived "on the bayou" all of his life. Across the bayou lived a fellow named Clarence. They never liked each other from the time they were little boys. They used to yell at one another across the bayou and threaten to beat each other up. Neither one could swim so they could not get across to settle the dispute. The yells and threats continued on well into their adult lives.

Even as grown men their animosity grew towards each other. They both married and continued to live where they grew up. Boudreaux chose Chlotilde for his wife, and, although she did not understand his ill-feelings, she supported him. Boudreaux would holler at Clarence that he would beat him up, and Clarence would shout the same warning right back at Boudreaux. This went on everytime they saw one another.

Finally, one day the parish began building a bridge across the bayou. This project took two years to complete. When it was finished, Boudreaux looked at Chlotilde and said, "Ya kno, beb, all my life Clarence been tellin' me dat he gonna beat me up. Well, taday he goin' have his chance. Me dere, ahm goin' cross dat bridge and we goin' settle dis ting once and fo' all."

Chlotilde looked at him and said, "Well Boudreaux, a man got ta do wat a man got ta do."

Boudreaux walked out of his house and headed for the bridge. As he was crossing it, he stopped, looked up, turned around and ran back home.

Chlotilde was quite surprised to see him so soon and asked, "May, sha, wat's da matta. How come ya back so quick, you? Ah taut ya wuz goin' ta beat up dat Clarence fella?"

"Haw yeah, ah wuz. But ah chenged my mind, me," answered Boudreaux.

"May why?" inquired Chlotilde.

"Well, me dere, ah start ta cross dat bridge ya kno and ah look up. Den ah see dis great big sign dat say, 'Clarence - 13 feet, 9 inches.' Chooooo, he sho din look dat big from dis side da bayou, non! Ah ain't goin' mess wit him, me!"

A Way With Words

Boudreaux was eventually weeded out of the Paratroopers so he was assigned as a special assistant to the captain of his platoon.

"Boudreaux," he said, "we just found out that Robichaux's wife suffered a severe heart attack and didn't make it. You better go tell him."

Boudreaux walked into the barracks, stuck his head through the door and shouted, "Hey Robichaux, yo' ole lady jis had da big one and she done croked!"

The captain was horrified. "Boudreaux, that's no way to tell a man bad news! I think we'd better send you to Tact and Diplomay School for some sensitivity training."

"May okay, if you tink ah really need it, me," said Boudreaux. So he spent a year studying at Tact and Diplomay School. On the day he returned, the captain approached him.

"Well, Boudreaux, how did you do in school?" asked the captain.

"Chooooo, good, good!" answered Boudreaux. "Da top o' da class! Ah really learn some tack, me."

"I'm glad to hear that," said the captain, "because Guilbeau's wife was just killed in a really bad car accident and I want you to break the news to him."

Boudreaux entered the barracks, paused at the doorway and called all the men to attention. When they were lined up, he stepped before them and ordered, "All doze whose wife is still living, take one step ta da front....whooop, not so fas dere, Guilbeau!"

Long Distance Love

Boudreaux and Chlotilde were having some problems in their relationship. They just couldn't seem to get along and would fuss and fight all the time. It was suggested that they receive marriage counseling. Boudreaux called to make an appointment. In their telephone conversation the psychologist related that the problem might be due to stress. Being a jogger, he knew how helpful that activity was in relieving stress. So the psychologist suggested to Boudreaux that he try jogging to resolve the matter before they went into counseling.

Boudreaux said, "Ya kno someting doc, ahm not dat much on axercise, me, but if dat kin save my marriage dere, ahm willing ta try it. Ah sho luv dat woman, me! How far ya tink ah ought ta jog?"

"Try ten miles a day," said the doctor.

"Caaaaaw, tan mile a day!" exclaimed Boudreaux. "Dat goin' be tuff, but ahm goin' try my bess, me. How offen ya tink ah should run?" asked Boudreaux.

"Try it every day for a couple of weeks," said the doctor, "then call me and let me know how you're getting along."

True to his word, fourteen days later Boudreaux telephoned the doctor and said, "Hey doc, me dere, ah done zackly watchu told me ta do. Arry day fo' da last foteen days ah done struggle trew dem tan mile."

The doctor asked, "Well Boudreaux, did it help your relationship with Chlotilde?"

"Huh, how ahm posta kno, me. Ahm stuck here a hundred forty miles from da house!"

Horsing Around

Chlotilde was checking Boudreaux's pants pockets as she was putting them in the washing machine. She pulled out a piece of paper that had "Mary Lou" written on it and what appeared to be a telephone number. Needless to say, she was quite upset and confronted Boudreaux.

"Oh Boudreaux!" shouted Chlotilde. "Ya foolin' round on me, you? Look at wat ah found dere in yo pocket! 'Spleen dat ta me!"

Examining the contents of the paper Boudreaux replied, "Aw beb, it's nutting. Me and Shawee, we, went ta da race track las week and dat wuz da neem o' da hoss dat ah bet on and all da numbas ah needed ta place da bet."

Chlotilde accepted his explanation and calmed down. A few days later the phone rang and she answered it. Chlotilde turned to Boudreaux, gave him a pair of eyes and said, "It's fo' you. Yo hoss wanna talk witchu!"

Beauty And The Beast

Boudreaux took Chlotilde and their son, Junya, to the big city for the first time. Upon arriving in New Orleans, they went to the tallest building they could find. Naturally, Chlotilde was fascinated by all the shops and immediately began browsing in them. Boudreaux and Junya began walking around in the lobby and came to these two big, golden doors.

"Caaaaaw, Junya, looka da size o' dem doors!" exclaimed Boudreaux. "Ah wonda ware dey go and wat dey do?"

"Ah don't kno, me," said Junya as he looked on in amazement.

As they were looking at the doors, an old, ugly woman approached. She pushed a button, the doors opened, she entered and the doors closed. Boudreaux and Junya could see the numbers above the doors begin to change: 1........2........3........stop, pause, and then start to come down: 3........2........1........The doors open and out walked a beautiful, young, voluptuous woman.

"Chooooo, Poppa! Didja see dat? Dat old, ugly woman went into dat box and wuz chenged into a beautiful young lady!" marveled Junya.

"Haw yeah, son! Ah seed dat, me. Quick, go run git yo mama!" instructed Boudreaux.

Angelic Thought

Boudreaux and T-Boy were sitting on the front porch. Said T-Boy, "Ya kno, Boudreaux. Ahm a lucky man, yeah, me."

"Watchu mean?" questioned Boudreaux.

"My wife dere, she's an angel, yeah," explained T-Boy.

"Huh, you lucky, you," said Boudreaux. "Mine's still living!"

Silence Is Golden

Boudreaux suspected Chlotilde was having a hearing problem. One night he was across the room from her while her back was turned.

Softly he asked, "Kin ya hear me, sha?" He heard only silence.

He repeated the question with no response. Coming closer, Boudreaux asked again, "Oh beb, kin ya hear me now?"

Finally, he walked directly behind the chair Chlotilde was in and asked again if she could hear him.

She gave him an exasperated sigh, "Fo' da fort time, Boudreaux, yeah ah kin hear ya!"

Closely Related

"Ah got me a lil riddle fo' you dere, Boudreaux," said Shawee.

"May okay," said Boudreaux.

"Wat's da difference between a pit bull and Chlotilde wit PMS?"

"Lipstick?" answered a reflective Boudreaux.

Lost Business

Chlotilde could not wait to share the news of her anniversary gift to Boudreaux.

Said Chlotilde, "Dis is our tirtiet wedding anniversary, and ah bought dis lil house wit da two dolla ah charge ya arrytime ah took ya ta bed. Do you like it, beb?"

112

"It's not bad, Chlotilde, not too bad atall," said Boudreaux reservedly.

"Wat's da matta, Boudreaux?" asked Chlotilde. "Ya don't sound too happy, you."

"Oh, ahm happy, sha, but —- ah wuz jis tinking, me," replied Boudreaux.

"Bot wat?" questioned Chlotilde.

"Bot how big dis house would be if ahda gave ya all my bidness," answered Boudreaux.

Strange Apparel

Boudreaux and his podnas had spent the night at the camp to go duck hunting the next morning. Rising early, they began to dress for the day's activity.

As they were dressing Shawee looked at Boudreaux in amazement and asked,
"May Boudreaux, how long ya been waring a girdle, you?"

"Huh, arry since Chlotilde found it in da glove compartment o' my caw!" replied Boudreaux.

You just might be a Cajun if ...

You give up Tabasco for Lent.

You start an angel food cake with a roux.

You think playing Bingo every week is a direct contribution to the church.

You think banning church fairs is a sacrilege.

Chapter 12

Boudreaux on Spiritual Matters

The Religious Thing To Do

Boudreaux had just returned from a boudin-making conference in Canada and stopped by to see his podna, Cowan. "How wuz yo trip, Boudreaux?" asked Cowan. "Wuz it wert da effort ta go?"

"Haw yeah! Ah learn some stuff, me!" said Boudreaux. "Ah kin make some boudin all kina ways now. Da only bad ting, dough, wuz da trip back home."

"May wat happened?" inquired Cowan.

"We wuz cruising at abot tirty tousand feet in dat saven-forty-saven wen we hit one o' dem big arr pocket," explained Boudreaux. "Pooooo, dat pleen drop abot a thousand feet in no time atall."

"Caaaaaw, dat's someting, yeah!" said Cowan in amazement.

"And den, dey had jis serve us one o' dem great meals, ya kno, so dere wuz food flying in da arr, papers scattered all ova da place and da pleen wuz shaking planny planny," continued Boudreaux. "Arrybody wuz scared, yeah. Pooooo! Me dere, ah almost ruined a perfectly good pare o' undawares."

"May ah guess so!" said a sympathetic Cowan. "Den wat happpened?"

"Chooooo!" said Boudreaux excitedly. "Da people wuz holling and screaming and finally one lady, she stood up and yell, 'Quick, somebody do someting religious!' So me dere, being a good Catlic, ah jump up outa my seat and pass a collection. Ta tell da troot, it din do too much ta calm dem down, but ah got me tirteen dollas and tirty-five sants! And it sho felt good ta do someting religious in a time o' need!"

A Cold Conclusion

Boudreaux had a dream that he had died and gone to hell. The devil greeted him at the doorway and immediately turned up the heat.

"How do you like that?" asked the devil.

"Ta tell da troot, sha," replied Boudreaux, "it's lika normal summa day in Sot Loseiana. Ah kinda feel at home, me."

This annoyed the devil so he turned up the heat even more. "Now how do you feel?" he asked.

"Chooooo, it feel like wen ah hunt teal in da marsh. In fac, it make me feel like ahm in heaven," said Boudreaux.

This really aggravated the devil so he kept turning up the heat but with the same results. So he decided to use reverse psychology. He turned down the thermostat so that it got extremely cold causing ice cycles to form all around. He looked at Boudreaux and said, "Tell me, how do you feel now?"

Boudreaux responded, "Pooooo, ahm a little cold and miserable but ah ain't naver been so happy in my whole life, me."

"How can you be happy? " asked the devil.

"Cuz da New Orleans Saints done won da Super Bowl!" said Boudreaux.

"What makes you think that?" asked the devil.

"Maaaaay, cuz arrybody say dat da Saints ain't goin' win da Super Bowl til hell freeze ova!"

Strange Teacher

Boudreaux was leaning against his lawnmower when the parish priest, Father Raoul, came by.

"You look so sad, Boudreaux. What's wrong?" asked the good Father.

"Ah jis wish ah had me a bike instead o' dis doggone lawnmotor," explained Boudreaux.

"Tell you what," said the priest, "I've got a bike and I'd be happy to trade with you."

The exchange took place. The next day as Boudreaux was

riding his bike near the church rectory, he noticed Father Raoul repeatedly cranking the lawnmower.

"Wat's da matta dere, Padre?" asked Boudreaux.

"This lawnmower just won't start," replied Father.

"Lemme tellya someting, Fadda," said Boudreaux. "Dat machine is a lil tampermantal. Ya jis gotta cuss at it ta git it goin'," explained Boudreaux.

"But I don't know how to cuss," said Father.

"Sha, you jis keep crankin' da way ya doing and you goin' learn in a hurry, yeah!" warned Boudreaux.

No Good Deed Goes Unrewarded

Boudreaux stood at the gates of heaven when St. Peter stopped him and said, "Oh, no. You don't get into Heaven anymore just for being good. You have to have done something truly great. Have you done anything that you can say is really and truly great in your lifetime.

"Haaaaaw yeah!" said Boudreaux. "Ah saw dis group o' Hell's Angels giving dis ole lady a real hard time ya kno, so me dere, ah kick ova da leader's bike, slap him up side da haid and spit in his face."

"That's great!" St. Peter said. "When did you do that?"

Glancing at his watch Boudreaux said, "Uuuuuh, 'bot teree minutes ago!"

Unjust Reward

Boudreaux and Kymon died and went to heaven. Meeting St. Peter at the Pearly Gates Boudreaux said, "May Pete, how you been, beb?"

"All right," said St. Peter, "but I've got some pretty bad news for you, Boudreaux. You've been so bad on earth that your punishment will be to spend all eternity with an ugly woman."

"Sha Lawd!" said a dejected Boudreaux. "Ah finely got away from Chlotilde, me, and den ah got ta git mysef stuck wit a ugly woman. Dat sho is discouraging, yeah. But if ah hafto, ahm jis goin' try ta make da bess o' it, me."

The next day Boudreaux and his ugly woman were walking down the golden street in heaven when he saw Kymon. He was shocked and confused to see him with the beautiful Cindy Crawford. Boudreaux decided to question St. Peter about this.

"Yo, Pete. Ah tink we got us a lil mistake here, bro," said Boudreaux. "Ah got me dis lil question fo' ya dat ah tink kin clare up dis whol' ting. How come, me dere, ahm stuck wit dis ugly woman, uuuuugly as sin, and Kymon, who wuz mo' worser den me in real life, him, he git Cindy Crawford? How kin dat be?"

"Well, Boudreaux," said St. Peter, "you just don't understand. Cindy Crawford's punishment is to spend eternity with Kymon!"

Through My Fault...

Shawee and Boudreaux were taking Boudreaux's uncle, the Catholic priest, on a tour of the French Quarters. As they made their way through the Quarters, they stumbled upon a strip joint. Naturally, Boudreaux wanted to go in and check it out. But Shawee, realizing who was with them said, "Ah non, Boudreaux. We can't do dat! We got da priest wit us. Watchu tinking abot, you?"

"May, you rat, yeah, Shawee. Tank ya fo' bringin' dat ta my attantion."

"Hey," said Father Boudreaux, "lemme tell bote o' yall someting, dere. Jis cuz a man's on a diet don't mean he can't look at da menu, non!"

Narrow Gates

Ole Boudreaux died and was trying to get into heaven. When he reached the Pearly Gates, St. Peter said, "Look Boudreaux, there is an additional requirement for getting into heaven. It is now necessary to pass a spelling test."

"May, okay," responded Boudreaux. "Ahm not too too bad in spelling, me. Gimme dat furst word, dere."

"Spell 'cat'," said St. Peter.

"Chooooo! Dis goin' be easy as eatin' a piece o' boudin. C-a-t," spelled Boudreaux confidently.

"Good," remarked St. Peter. "Now spell 'dog'."

"D-o-g," said a smiling Boudreaux.

"Right again," St. Peter replied. "Now for your last word. Spell 'rat'."

"Whew! Tank God ah spant dat extra year in da tird grade, me. Dis is so easy ah kin hardly belief it. R-a-t," said Boudreaux with a puffed chest.

"Correct. You pass with flying colors, so come on in," said St. Peter. "I have a little heavenly business to take care of for a few minutes, so would you mind standing at the Gates and giving the test to anyone who wants to enter?"

"May, no prablum, sha. Take yo' time. Arryting's unda control here," said Boudreaux proudly.

Lo and behold, the first one to show up at the Pearly Gates is Boudreaux's wife, Chlotilde. She was quite surprised but delighted to see him as the "keeper of the keys" at the Gates.

Said Chlotilde excitedly, "Boudreaux, it's so good ta see ya agin and ta tink dat we kin spand da rest o' our lives togetta in eternity. Haaaaaw, ahm so happy, me!"

"Hol on dere, Chlotilde. Not so fas! Tings done chenge a lil bit aroun' here, yeah," cautioned Boudreaux. "Now ya gotta pass a spelling tess ta git in."

"Dat don't make no matta," beamed Clothilde. "Gimme dat first word, sha, so ah kin git trew dem Gate and be witchu."

"May okay, beb. Spell Tchoupitoulas!" said Boudreaux.

Holy Visit

The Pope had heard much about Boudreaux and his escapades and decided that he wanted to meet him. So His Excellency faxed Boudreaux asking him to come to the Vatican for a visit. Needless to say, he was excited and wanted to share the news with his best friend, Shawee.

"Man, Shawee. Dat's some excitin', yeah, ta kno dat da Pope kno who ah am, me! Butchu kno wat? Ah don't tink ahm goin' go," said Boudreaux.

"May how come?" asked Shawee.

"Cuz ah don't kno how ta talk Polish, me, and ah sho don't want ta embarrass mysef wit da Pope," responded Boudreaux.

"Dat's no prablum," said a helpful Shawee. "Dat's a long arrpleen ride ova dere and ya kin learn arryting ya need ta kno on da way. Dey pass out dem headphone while da pleen is in da arr and ya kin learn arryting abot da language ya need ta kno ta git by."

"May, tank ya, sha, fo' dat information. Dat sound lika real good idear, yeah," responded Boudreaux.

Boudreaux bought his ticket and headed for Rome. Enroute the flight attendant asked if he wanted a pair of headphones, just like Shawee said she would.

"Haw, yeah, ah want a pare o' dem, me," answered Boudreaux without hesitation. She instructed him to plug them in and put them over his ears. He did so immediately and continued to listen all the way to Rome.

Upon arrival at the airport, the Pope greeted him at the gate. Said the Pope, "Well, Mr. Boudreaux, after all this time I finally get to meet you. Tell me, how are you doing?"

And Boudreaux answered, "Scheeeeeeeeeeeeeeeeeeeeeeeeeeee!"

Burnt Chicken

Rocking on Boudreaux's front porch, T-Brud turned to him and said, "You kno Boudreaux, it sho is tarrible wat dey doing in da sout, yeah."

"May, watchu mean?" quizzed Boudreaux.

"Chooooo, you mean ya don't kno, you? Man dey burning down all da churches ova dere!" responded T-Brud.

"It don't make no matta ta me, non," said Boudreaux. "Ah like Popeye's mo betta anyhow!"

Versed In The Faith

Boudreaux, Shawee and Cowan died and were at the Pearly Gates. St. Peter meets them and informs them that they can enter heaven if they can answer one simple question.

"Dat can't be dat hard," said Boudreaux. "Between da teree o' us ah kno fo' sho dat we kin come up wit da ansa. Go head Pete, give us yo bess shot, sha."

"The question is," said St. Peter, "what is Easter?"

"Aw dat's so easy," said Shawee. "It's da holiday in Novamba wen arryone git togedda, eat turkey and are tankful."

"Wrong!" replied St. Peter and proceeds to ask Cowan the same question.

"Ah kno, me," said Cowan. "Easta is dat holiday in Desamba wen we all put up a nice tree, exchange presents and salabrate da bert o' Jesus."

St. Peter looks at him and shakes his head in disgust. He turns to Boudreaux and asks, "What is Easter?"

Boudreaux smiles, looks St. Peter in the eye and says, "Ah can't belief dem udda two guys, me. Dey musta ducked outa Catechism class, dem. Easta is da Christian holiday dat coincide wit da Jewish salabration o' da Passova. Jesus and his disciples dere wuz eatin' da las suppa wen he wuz double crossed by one o' dem and turned ova ta da Rumans. Da Rumans took him ta be crucified. Dey stab him in da side, made him ware a crown o' torns and den hung him on da cross. Den he wuz buried in a cave which wuz sealed off wit a big big rock. Arry year dey move dat big rock back so dat Jesus kin come out, and if he see his shadow, him, dere goin' be six mo' week o' winta!"

And Now For The Starting Lineup...

From the time they were young boys on the bayou, Boudreaux and Shawee played baseball. They shared a passion for the game that was unequaled by anyone. Both continued playing even into their adult years and followed the sport with zeal and excitement.

Shawee died and left Boudreaux without a companion to participate with in his favorite sport. A couple of weeks later, Boudreaux was sitting on his front porch really feeling down. He missed his baseball podna. He just sat there staring into space tossing the ball repeatedly into his glove. Suddenly, he heard a voice whisper, "Boudreaux, Boudreaux." Although he didn't see anyone, he recognized the voice. It was Shawee.

"Shawee, is datchu?" asked Boudreaux.

"Haw yeah, it's me, all rat," answered Shawee.

"Now ah kin fine out someting ah all da time wanted ta kno, me, arry since ah wuz a lil boy. Do dey play baseball in heaven, Shawee?" inquired Boudreaux.

"Dey sho do," replied Shawee.

"Dat's so good ta kno, yeah," said a relieved Boudreaux. "Ah feel mo' betta now. But watchu doing here, you?"

"Ah come ta bring ya some good news and some bad news," continued Shawee. "Da good news is dat we got us da bestest fields, da prettiest grasses and most expansive equipment in heaven."

"May wat could be da bad news?" asked Boudreaux.

"Da bad news, sha," answered Shawee, "is dat you scheduled ta pitch tamorra nite, you!"

Ready To Build

As a young boy Boudreaux went to confession with Father Raoul. "Bless me Fadda fo' ah have sinned," said Boudreaux. "Ah stole me some lumba."

"My son, you know it's wrong to steal," said Father. "For your penance you are to pray three Our Fathers."

One week later Boudreaux went to confession again. "Bless me Fadda fo' ah have sinned," said Boudreaux. "Ah stole me some mo' lumba."

"My son, this is a serious matter," said Father. "For your penance you are to pray the Rosary."

Another week goes by and here comes Boudreaux again.

"Bless me Fadda fo' ah have sinned," confessed Boudreaux. "Ah took anudda big pile o' lumba, dere."

"This is getting out of hand!" exclaimed Father. "For your penance I want you to make a novena."

"Okay Fadda, if you got da blueprint, ah got da lumba, me," replied Boudreaux.

On A Personal Basis

Boudreaux died and was trying to get into heaven. St. Peter was waiting for him at the Pearly Gates and informed him that he would have to answer one of three questions in order to enter. He began the series of questions.

"How many seconds are there in a year?" asked St. Peter.

"Twelve!" responded Boudreaux quickly and proudly.

"How do you get twelve?" asked a puzzled St. Peter.

"Well, dere's Januwary sacond, Fabruary sacond, March sacond and so fort," said Boudreaux.

"That's wrong," said St. Peter. "Here's your second question. How many days of the week begin with the letter 't'?"

"Fo'!" replied Boudreaux.

"What do you mean four?" asked a frustrated St. Peter.

"Well, dere's Chewsday, Tursday, taday and tamorra," smiled Boudreaux.

"That's ridiculous," said St. Peter. "Here's your last question, so take all the time you need. Here goes. What is God's name?"

"Ah don't need no time, me. Dat's so easy!" shouted Boudreaux. "It's Howard!"

"Howard!" exclaimed St. Peter. "How did you ever come up with such an absurd idea as that?"

"Maaaaay, arry nite wen ah say my prayers, me, ah say 'our Fadda, who art in heaven, Howard be dy neem," said Boudreaux.

You just might be a Cajun if...

You use a gill net to play tennis, badminton or volleyball in your back yard.

You're asked to name the Fab Four and answer, "Paul Prudhomme, John Folse, Justin Wilson and Vernon Roger."

Your idea of a seven course meal is a six pack of beer and a platter of crawfish.

You think lobster is a crawfish on steroids.

Chapter 13

Boudreaux On Sports & Recreation

That's What Friends Are For

Boudreaux came into a lot of money and was bragging to Shawee that he was going to build three swimming pools.

"May ah kin undastand ya wanting a swamming pool, but how come teree pools, Boudreaux?" asked Shawee.

"Maaaaay, one got cold wata, one got warm wata and da udda one got no wata atall," replied Boudreaux.

"Da one wit cold wata ah can undastand, me," said Shawee. "Ah kin even go along wit da one wit da warm wata. But how come ya want a pool wit no wata atall? Dat don't make no sanse, non!"

"Sha Lawd," said Boudreaux, "you'd be some surprised, yeah, ta kno how many o' my frans don't kno how ta swam."

Sign Language

T-Boy shouted to Boudreaux, "Ah taut yall wuz goin' watch Skip Bertman's LSU Tigers play baseball dis aftanoon?"

"May, we did go, yeah," said Boudreaux.

"Fo sho? Den how come yall here rat now?" asked T-Boy.

"Cuz me and Shawee wuz driving on da I-10 in Baton Rouge and we come ta dis big, big sign dat say, LSU - Left." said Boudreaux. "May, ahm not stoopid, me. Ya don't tink ahm gonna go if dey ain't dere? So we turn aroun' and come home, us!"

No Stroke Of Sympathy

Boudreaux was playing golf with his uncle, the priest and Dr. Fontenot. They were waiting for a particularly slow moving group of golfers on the fairway to hole #7.

Boudreaux was getting very aggravated, as usual, and said,

"Maaaaay, wat's da matta wit dese guys? My grandma wuz sleaux, but she wuz planny old, her! We been here waiting fo' twanny or tirty minutes na."

Dr. Fontenot said, "I've never seen such poor, slow play."

"Here comes the greenskeeper," said the padre. "Let's ask him what's going on."

"Hey, Charlie, what's with those guys ahead of us? They're kind of slow, aren't they?" questioned the priest.

"Yes, but that's a group of blind fire fighters," replied Charlie. "They lost their sight while saving our clubhouse from burning last year. Out of gratitude, we let them play anytime they want free of charge."

The threesome were taken by surprise and quite moved by the explanation. The priest said, "That's so sad. I think I'll say a special prayer for them tonight."

"That's a great idea," said the doctor. "And I'm going to contact my opthalmologist buddy and see if there's anything he can do for them."

Not to be outdone with sympathy, Boudreaux offered, "Sha Lawd, ah don't kno, me, how come dem guys jis can't play at nite?"

Best Seat In The House

Boudreaux's football coach was always trying to exercise his players' minds by asking them what they would do under certain conditions in an important game.

Walking the sideline one day, he stopped where Boudreaux was sitting and asked, "Boudreaux, if it was third down and 25 yards to go, and we were on our own 20 yard line, what would you do?"

"Maaaaay, ahd move ta da udda side o' da bench, me, so ah could see da play mo' betta!" replied Boudreaux.

Bad Timing

Boudreaux and Chlotilde went on vacation to England. They decided to take a tour and ended up in one of the large cathedrals.

As the tour guide was highlighting some of the significant events of this historic place, she said, "And this is where they signed the Magna Carta."

Boudreaux looked at her and asked, "And wen dey did dat, sha?"

Said the tour guide, "1215."

Looking at his watch Boudreaux exclaimed, "Caaaaaw, dat's some bad luck, yeah, beb! We missed it by only twanny minutes."

Full Of Compassion

Boudreaux, Shawee, Cowan and T-Brud were playing a round of golf with a $200 wager on the match. Boudreaux had a 10-foot putt on the 18th green to win the money. He eyed the break from every angle and was meticulous in setting up to stroke the ball. As he was settling in his stance for the putt, a funeral procession started to pass. Boudreaux put down his putter, took off his cap, placed it over his chest, and waited for the funeral procession to pass. After the last vehicle was out of sight, Boudreaux picked up his putter and resumed his putting stance.

Seeing this, Shawee said in amazement, "May sha, dat wuz da mos touching ting ah naver did see befo', me. Wit da match on da line, ah can't bleave you stopped playing ta pay yo respects! Wat a decent ting ta do, Boudreaux!"

"Yabbut, Chlotilde wuz a good woman, yeah," replied Boudreaux. "We wuz married fo' 25 years, us!"

New Found Strength

The circus came to the bayou country and was an immediate hit. One of the main attractions was a wrestler called the "Alligator Man." He was so good that the management offered a $1000.00 cash prize to anyone who could wrestle and defeat him. This sounded like both a challenge and an opportunity to Shawee, T-Boy, Cowan and Kymon. So they persuaded their podna, Boudreaux, to meet the challenge and get into the ring with him.

But all of his buddies cautioned him, "Wataver ya do, Boudreaux, wen ya wrasslin' dat fella be sho you don't-let-him-gitchu-in-da famous 'alligata hold!' Cuz sha, if ya do, it's all ova but da crying, yeah. He not only goin' beatchu, he's gonna hurtchu. So be on da lookout!"

Boudreaux courageously climbed into the ring and began to wrestle the famed "Alligator Man." Within minutes the two men were wrapped around each other. Their bodies were so twisted and intertwined that you couldn't tell what body part belonged to who. As his podnas watched closely, they saw Boudreaux go down on the mat with the "Alligator Man" on top of him. With Boudreaux caught in the powerful "alligator hold," they quickly closed their eyes to avoid seeing the inevitable.

While their eyes were still closed, they heard a loud scream and scrambling around. Opening their eyes they saw Boudreaux on top and the "Alligator Man" pinned to the mat. They heard the referee count loud and clear: one, two, three! It was all over and Boudreaux had won!

Stunned, his podnas asked, "May Boudreaux, wat happened? How ya got outa dat "alligata hold", you? Nobody done naver done dat befo'!"

Boudreaux replied, "Chooooo man! Me and him wuz all twisted togedda ya kno. And when ah look up all ah kin see dere in front of me is a nombrie (navel). So ah figure dat my only chance ta break dat hold is ta bite it. So ah bite down on dat nombrie as hard as ah kin, me. Sha Lawd! You got any idear, you, how much strent a man kin git wen he bite his own nombrie?"

Foot Compass

Returning to his seat at a New Orleans Zephers' baseball game, Boudreaux asked a lady seated on the aisle, "'Scuse me, beb. Did ah stap on yo' foot wen ah lef, me?"

"Why, yes you did, sir," smiled the lady ready to accept an apology.

"Whew, tank God," said Boudreaux, "den ah kno ahm on da rat row!"

Small World

Boudreaux and Gaston were playing a round of golf and were behind a very slow female twosome. The ladies were constantly hitting in the rough and taking a long time to locate their ball. Gaston decided he would ask them if they would allow him and Boudreaux to play through. Before reaching them, he quickly turned the cart around and headed back towards his playing partner.

"Wat's da matta?" asked Boudreaux. "You look like ya done seen a ghost, you!"

"Whew, wat a close call!" exclaimed Gaston. "As ah approached da ladies, ah wuz able ta recanize dem. It wuz my wife and my mistress. Tank God dey din see me!"

"Look," said Boudreaux. "We can't keep playing dis slo. Tellya wat. Ahm goin' go talk ta dem ta see if dey goin' lettus play through."

Boudreaux took off and, just like Gaston, quickly turned around and headed back.

Reaching Gaston, Boudreaux said, "Sha Lawd, its a small world, yeah!"

High Flying Cajun

Boudreaux served in the Army and was selected for the Paratroopers. After extensive training, he still was not too confident about jumping out of a perfectly good airplane. The big day came when they were to make their first jump. The sergeant reviewed the procedures very carefully with his new recruits.

Said the sergeant to his nervous men, "Listen guys. It's really very simple. Jump out of the plane, yell 'Geronimo' and then pull the ripcord on your parachute."

Boudreaux was still uncertain about jumping, so he went to the back of the line. One at a time, all the men in front of him jumped. When he got to the door, Boudreaux still had second thoughts, so he hesitated for a moment. Without warning, his sergeant pushed him out of the plane and slammed the door shut.

About ten seconds later there was a loud thump, thump, thump, thump coming from the outside of the airplane. Puzzled, the sergeant opened the door to see what was making the noise. There to his surprise and amazement was Boudreaux flapping his arms wildly and yelling, "May wat's da neem o' dat injun agin, sha?"

Gutter Ball

"Sha Lawd. Ahm sho nuff discouraged yeah, me," said Boudreaux. "Ah done lost fo' balls taday. Ah tink ahm goin' quit da game."

"Dat's not too bad," said Gaston. "A lotta gulfers loose fo' balls in one day."

"Yeah, but me dere, ahm a bowler!" corrected Boudreaux.

Lean Cuisine

"Hey Boudreaux," said Cowan. "Ah hear dat you jis got back from yo vacation in Florida. How wuz it, man?"

"May, okay," answered Boudreaux. "Arryting wuz real good 'cept fo'one ting."

"And wat's dat?" asked Cowan.

"Da food dere wuz tarrible!" explained Boudreaux. "Da mash potatoes dey wuz watery, da green beans din got no taste atall, da roast beef wuz tuff like shoe ledda, da apple pie wuz gooey and slimy, and da coffee taste a whole lot like some dishwata."

"Caaaaaw, dat's bad, yeah!" said a surprised Cowan.

"Butchu kno wat da most worstest ting o' all wuz?" asked Boudreaux.

"Wat?" asked Cowan.

"Sha, dey gave ya such lil bitty servings!" responded Boudreaux.

Time On My Side

"Man, ah sho wish we hurry up and go back to Daylight Saving Time, me," said Boudreaux. "Cuz it goin' hep my gulf game out a lot."

"May how kin dat hep yo' game?" inquired T-boy.

"Cuz wit dat extra hour, dere, ah got me mo time ta look fo' my ball in da ruff," explained Boudreaux.

Boat For Sale

"Hey, Boudreaux," shouted T-Boy, "ya got dis sign in yo front yard dat say "Boat For Sale" but ah don't see no boat, me. All ah see dere, me, is a pirogue and a shotgun. How come ya lie like dat, you?"

"Maaaaay," answered Boudreaux, "wat's da matta witchu, T-Boy? Ya stoopid or someting, you? Dat pirogue and dat shotgun dere, dey bote fo' sale, dem!"

You just might be a Cajun if...

You're flying for the first time, and you're so happy when that plane touches down on the driveway.

When the pilot announces that beverage service is now available in the cabin and you open your ice chest and pull out a Dixie beer.

When boarding the airplane you stop by the cockpit, give the pilot an ice chest of shrimp and ask how the family is.

You know the difference between Zatarains, Zydeco and Zeringue.

Chapter 14

Boudreaux On Technology

Computer Whiz

Boudreaux went to the local photographer, Cheramie, with an old snapshot of his father.

"Kin ya enlarge dis pitcher fo' me?" asked Boudreaux.

"May dat's no prablum," said Cheramie. "Wit dese new computa dere, ah kin do most annyting."

"Ah got me a lil fava ta axe you. Wen you enlarge it, kin ya take off Poppa's moostache?" asked Boudreaux. "Dat wuz a long time ago wen he had dat, and he don't look da seem wit it."

"No prablemo," replied Cheramie.

"Come ta tink o' it," said Boudreaux, "ah don't naver remamber Poppa wit a hat on his haid nedda. Ya tink ya kin redo dat pitcher witout da hat?"

"Shaaaaa, dat goin' be as easy as eatin' a piece o' lost bread," responded Cheramie.

"Jis one lil ting, Boudreaux," said Cheramie. "Do ya remember which side da haid yo poppa part his hairs?"

"Huh, if da computa is as good as you say, den wen ya take off his hat you goin' be able ta see dat fo' yosef!" laughed Boudreaux.

Low Tech Guru

Boudreaux and T-Brud were having a few cold ones at the Hubba Hubba when the conversation turned to technology.

"Man, ah jis got connected ta dat Innaneck, me. Talk abot someting!" said T-Brud. "Pooooo! Dey got all kina stuff on dere, yeah. But it don't make no sanse ta me."

"May watchu mean?" asked Boudreaux.

"All dem term dey use, ah don't kno wat dey mean, non," replied T-Brud.

"Ah kno a lil bit abot dat, yeah. Go head and axe me watchu want," offered Boudreaux.

"Wat's dis 'auxiliary power'?" asked T-Brud.

"Maaaaay, dat's jis a good shot o' Jack Daniels!" explained Boudreaux.

"And 'backup'?" queried T-Brud.

"Sha, dat's watchu do wen ya come face ta face wit an alligata," said Boudreaux. "And ya do it in a hurry, yeah!"

"Den how bot da 'bar code'?" continued T-Brud.

Said Boudreaux, "Dem's da fighting rules at da Hubba Hubba."

"Man you kno' some stuff, you," said an impressed T-Brud. "But wat abot 'bug'?

"Huh, dat's da axcuse ya use wen you call in sick," answered Boudreaux.

"Well, wat's dis 'cache'?" continued T-Brud.

"May, dat's watchu gotta use wen ya run outa da food stamp," said a proud Boudreaux.

"Den wat's dis 'fax'?" asked T-Brud.

"Dat's watchu lie abot wen ya git da audit from da IRS!" laughed Boudreaux.

"Ahm jis so imprassed, me, wit watchu kno'," said T-Brud. "Ah kin hardly wait ta git on da line agin ta use some o' dis stuff. But wat abot 'hacker'?"

"Well," answered Boudreaux, "dat's yo nonk Coon afta fifty-teree years o' smokin'. He's one o' da most worstest hackers ah kno, me."

"Dis one here scares me, yeah," admitted T-Brud. "Wat's 'megahertz'?"

"Dat's no big deal, dere," said Boudreaux. "All dat is is how yo haid feel da mornin' afta ya spant most o' da night drinkin' beer at da Hubba Hubba!"

"Wat's dis 'modem'?" asked a wide-eyed T-Brud.

"Dat's watchu do wen da grass git high!" answered Boudreaux. "Chooooo, ahm on a roll now, me. Hey bartander, bring us a coupla mo' Bud's ova here, sha. Wen ya hot ya hot, yeah!"

"Okay den, wat abot 'ROM'?" question T-Brud as he continued to take notes.

"Being a good Catlic ah sho taut ya would kno' dat one, you. Dat's da most easiest one o' dem all," said Boudreaux. "Couyon, dat's where da Pope live!"

"And wat's dis 'serial port'?" asked T-Brud.

"Dat's jis a gooood, red wine," countered Boudreaux licking his lips.

"Whew, all dis stuff jis bottles my mind," admitted T-Brud. "It can't take too much mo', non. Tank God ah jis got a coupla mo' fo' ya. All rat, now tell me abot dis 'superconductor'."

"Ya musta been raise in da boondock. You don't kno' nuttin', you. Dat's jis Amtrak's employee o' da year," responded a weary Boudreaux.

"Okay, jis one mo' den we trew," said T-Brud. "Wat's all dis talk abot 'windows', dere?" asked T-Brud.

"May dat's wat dem lil kid trow da rock at," answered a relieved Boudreaux.

"Shaaaaa, ah kno' some stuff now, me," slurred T-Brud. "Wit all ah learned taday, dere, ah could probly try out fo' a job as da technical support person wit my local Innaneck provida. And on top o' dat, da beer wuz cold cold!"

"Yeah you rat, T-Brud. It don't git no betta den dis, non!" smiled Boudreaux as he guzzled his beer.

Nobody's Fool

"Hey, Boudreaux," said Gaston. "Ah hear you goin' ta da pirogue-makin' convantion in Ville Platte dis weekan'. Is dat a fac?"

"Haw yeah!" said Boudreaux. "Ahm goin' pass me a good time dere, sha. Man dey got some good lookin' wamans dat come from all ova da place!"

"You mean ya not bringin' Chlotilde witchu?" inquired Gaston.

"Sha Lawd, non," responded Boudreaux.

"May how come?" asked Gaston.

135

"Lemme axe ya dis. Woodju bring a peanut butta sandwich witchu if ya wuz goin' ta a banquet, you?" replied Boudreaux.

Nuisance Call

"Hey Boudreaux," said Kymon. "Ah hear ya goin' high class on me, huh sha?"

"May, watchu mean?" asked Boudreaux.

"T-boy told me datchu done got one o' dem caw phone installed. How ya like it?" inquired Kymon.

"Ta tell da troot, Kymon, it's a real peen in da tail." answered Boudreaux.

"May how come?" questioned Kymon.

"Sha Lawd, ahm so tired, me, o' running ta da garage arrytime dat talafoam ring!" explained Boudreaux.

Red Eye Special

Boudreaux had saved a lot of lumber and had it stacked behind his house. Hearing constant sawing and hammering going on, Shawee decided to discover what Boudreaux was doing.

"Boudreaux!" shouted Shawee. "Watchu doin' wit all dat wood and makin' all dat racket dere?"

"Haaaaaw, ahm building me a rocket ship," answered Boudreaux.

"A rocket ship!" exclaimed Shawee. "May fo' wat?"

"Ah done made up my mind, me, dat ahm goin' fly ta da sun!" said Boudreaux.

"Couyon! You stoopid, yeah, you," said Shawee. "You ain't naver goin' make it, non. Dat space ship goin' burn up wen it git close ta da sun!"

"Aw non! Not if ah go in da nite time!" said Boudreaux.

No Direction

Boudreaux and Cowan were driving "down the bayou" in Boudreaux's pickup truck when he suddenly pulled off the road.

"Ah ain't so sho dat my signal lights is workin', non," said Boudreaux. "Ahm goin' go out back, me, and ah wanchu ta turn dem on so ah kin check dem out."

Cowan put on the signal lights according to Boudreaux's instructions and waited. Boudreaux watched the back of the truck without saying a word.

An impatient Cowan yelled out, "Hey Boudreaux. Dey workin', sha?"

Boudreaux shouted back, "dey workin'....dey not workin'....dey workin'...., dey not workin'....dey workin'....dey not workin'."

Too Breezy

Boudreaux was taking his first helicopter ride to an oil rig in the Gulf in mid-January. It was extremely cold and he was shivering. After awhile, Boudreaux looked at the pilot and asked, "Sha, ya tink we could turn off dat big fan up dere fo' a lil while til ah warm up, me?"

Anxious To Help

An Englishman, a German and Boudreaux were scheduled to die with the guillotine. Each was asked to say his last words.

The Englishman was first and said "Long Live The Queen!" The blade was released but didn't fall, so he was released.

The German was next and said "Heil Hitler!" Again, the blade did not fall so he was set free, too.

Boudreaux stepped up proudly, pointed upward and announced, "You kno, sha, if you jis loosen dat big screw up dere a lil bit, dat blade gonna fall down arrytime, yeah!"

You just might be a Cajun if....

You're asked to name the four seasons and reply, "onions, celery, bell pepper and garlic."

Your mama announces each morning, "Well, I've got the rice cooking. Now what will we have for dinner?"

You let your black coffee cool and find it has gelled.

You're visiting with friends and get up to leave but continue talking for fifteen minutes as you stand by the sofa, another fifteen minutes by the doorway, an additional fifteen minutes while sitting in the car and then finish the conversation as you drive away.

Chapter 15

Boudreaux On Work

Ear Drop

Boudreaux and T-Brud were building a swing for the front porch and cutting the wood needed for the project. As Boudreaux guided the electric saw completely through the two by four and followed through, the saw continued upward in a circular motion and cut off his right ear.

Digging around in the sawdust, T-Brud found it, held it up and exclaimed, "Hey, Boudreaux, ah found it!"

Boudreaux looked at it and said, "Aw non. Dat's not mine, sha! My ear hada pancil behind it!"

Knee Deep In Work

Boudreaux and T-Boy were out looking for a job. They passed by a building with a sign that said, "Pilots Wanted."

"May, Boudreaux. You a pilot, you. Go in dere and git dat job," said T-Boy.

Boudreaux went inside and told the personnel director that he is a pilot with 20 years experience. The director immediately hired him. He came out and told T-Boy that he got the job.

"May, if you kin git dat job, den ah kin, too," said T-Boy. He went inside and talked with the personnel director.

"So, you're a pilot like Boudreaux? I really need more pilots," said the director.

"Aw non," said T-Boy, "ah shovel manure, me."

"Shovel manure?" said a puzzled director. "I'm sorry but I really have no need for someone who does that."

"Me dere, ahm a lil bit confused," said T-Boy. "Ya jis hired Boudreaux."

"Yes," responded the director, "but he's a pilot."

"But sha, ya don't undastand, you," explained T-Boy. "Ya see, ole Boudreaux, he can't pile it unless ah shovel it, me!"

What A Way To Go

Boudreaux and Gaston were casualties of the oil field bust in the 80's and decided to look for work in New Orleans. They quickly found jobs at the Dixie Brewery. After working only a couple of weeks, Boudreaux drowned in a beer vat. Management was quite upset over the incident and asked Gaston to return to the bayou and break the news to Chlotilde.

Upon hearing the news, Chlotilde inquired, "Gaston, did he suffa much, sha?"

"Ah don't tink so," answered Gaston. "In fac, he climb outa da vat teree times ta go ta da batrum!"

First Things First

Boudreaux was working with Cowan as a plumber's helper. On the very first morning, there was a job to be done in the men's restroom.

"Boudreaux, ya see dese two urinals, dere?" asked Cowan. "Dey outa orda, dem. Ah wanchu ta fix'em. Ahm goin' be back in an hour ta see how ya doing."

Sure enough, there was a sign over the urinals that read "Out of Order."

Wanting to make a good impression, Boudreaux tackled the job with enthusiasm. True to his word, Cowan returned an hour later.

"Oh Boudreaux, didja fix doze urinals," asked Cowan.

"Haw yeah!" said Boudreaux proudly. "Ah sho did, me. Dey wuz jis outa orda so, me dere, ah took da one on da lef and put it on da rat. Den ah took da one dat wuz on da rat and put it on da lef!"

Cajun Trailblazer

A lumber camp in the Pacific Northwest advertised that they were looking for a good lumberjack. Boudreaux saw the ad and went to apply in person.

The head lumberjack took one look at Boudreaux and said, "Man, you're not big enough for this kind of job. You're too short and way too skinny. You'd best go back home."

"May, all ah axe you is ta gimme a chance ta sho ya wat ah kin do, me," said Boudreaux.

"Alright well," said the lumberjack. "See that giant redwood tree over there? Take your axe and go cut it down."

Boudreaux headed for the tree and in five minutes was back knocking on the lumberjack's door.

"Ahm trew cuttin' down dat tree dere," said Boudreaux.

The lumberjack was amazed. He had never seen anyone cut down such a large tree so fast. "Where did you get the skill to chop down trees like that?" he asked.

"May, in da Sahara Forest," answered Boudreaux.

"You mean the Sahara Desert," said the lumberjack.

"Aw yeah! Dat's wat dey call it now!" said Boudreaux with tongue in cheek.

Like A Good Neighbor

Boudreaux called a carpenter in town and said that he needed him for a small job.

"Ah need me a lil box dere dat's two inches wide, two inches high, and fifty feet long. Kinya build dat fo' me?" asked Boudreaux.

The confused carpenter replied, "I can build it for you. That's no problem. But what in the world do you need that for?"

"Oh, it's not a big deal non, sha," responded Boudreaux. "It's jis dat my neighba moved abot a week ago and he fogot a coupla tings, him. So he axed me if ah could mail him his hose pipe."

141

No Halfway Job

The telephone company needed to install more telephone poles in a newly developed rural area. They decided to give the job to the contractor who could install them the fastest. They contacted Acme Pole Installers and a Cajun contractor by the name of Boudreaux to compete for the work.

The Acme Company was to work all day installing poles on one side of the road and Boudreaux and his crew were to handle the other side. At the end of the day the telephone company supervisor would check to see who would be awarded the job. Both groups worked feverishly all day. At sundown the supervisor checked their progress.

He sees that Acme has installed 24 poles during the course of the day and is very impressed. He looks at the other side of the road and sees that Boudreaux has installed only 4.

"Oh Boudreaux, why are you so slow?" asked the supervisor. "The other guys have done 24 already!"

"Aw yeah, dey mo' fasta all rat," responded Boudreaux, "but look how much dey lef sticking outa da ground, dem!"

Keep On Trucking

Boudreaux's house caught fire, and he quickly called the fire department. He was in a panic as he spoke to the chief.

"Chief! You betta git ova here rat away cuz my house is on fire, yeah!" shouted Boudreaux.

"Calm down, Boudreaux," said the chief. "How do we get to your house?"

"May, wat's da matta witchu?" inquired Boudreaux. "Yall don't got dem big red truck no mo'?"

Diesel Power

Boudreaux and Shawee found themselves out of work when the underwear factory in town shut down. Their boss informed them that they could go to the LSU (Louisiana State Unemployment) office, to see about applying for benefits.

Shawee waited as Boudreaux sat down at the desk for his interview.

"And what was your former occupation, sir?" asked the lady.

"Me dere, ah wuz a crotch stitcher. Ah specialized in ladies underpants," Boudreaux replied proudly.

The lady opened the manual with the benefit schedule, reviewed it and said, "Okay, you're eligible to receive $50.00 a week."

"Caaaaaw! Ya mean ah don't gotta do nuttin' and ah kin git $50.00 a week? Shaaaaa, dat's mo betta den eatin' a plate full o' crawfish etouffee!" exclaimed Boudreaux.

The lady turned her attention to Shawee and asked him the same question.

Shawee looked her straight in the eye and said, "Ah wuz a diesel fitter, me."

She looked in the manual again and said, "Very well. You're eligible for $200.00 a week in unemployment benefits."

"May wait jis a doggone minute dere!" shouted Boudreaux. "How come he goin' git $200.00 a week and me ahm only goin' git $50.00? Ah tolju dat ah usta be a crotch stitcher. Ya kno ya gotta be real good ta do dat kind o' work, yeah. All dem seams dey gotta be nice and straight and smood so dat nuttin' scratch you. And Shawee dere, him, he's only a diesel fitter and he gonna make at least twice mo' den me?"

"Oh," the lady replied, "but he's a skilled laborer with an education. Diesel fitters are in high demand expecially by oil field and heavy equipment users. There's not many diesel specialists around."

"Whoa, hol on dere, lady. Wait jis a minute," said Boudreaux. "Ya got it all wrong, you. Aw yeah, Shawee's a diesel fitter alrat. But wat dat mean is dat afta ah do all da fine work on da ladies' drawers, he pick dem up, look'um ova, stretch'em dis way and dat way, and den say, 'Aw yeah, dese'll fit her!'"

Cutting Corners

Boudreaux found himself in Washington on a tour of the White House with two other carpenters - one from Texas and the other from New York. The White House staff member was excited because the front gate was in need of repair and saw an opportunity to get it fixed.

He asked each one to give him an estimate of the cost. The carpenter from Texas pulled out a tape and measured the height and width of the gate. He took out a pocket calculator, punched in his figures and said it would cost $700.00 for materials and labor.

The fellow from New York went through the same process. He took out a ruler, measured, calculated and reported, "With materials and labor, the cost will be $900.00."

Boudreaux, without doing any measuring or calculation, immediately said that the job would cost $2700.00

The While House official said, "That's extremely high! And besides, how did you arrive at that price without doing any measuring or calculation?"

"May, it's simple, sha," responded Boudreaux. "A tousand dolla fo' me, a tousand fo' you, and we goin' hire da Texien fo' saven hundred dolla!"

To Nail Or Not To Nail

Boudreaux was remodeling his living room and was assisted by his good friend, Shawee. As Shawee was putting up the paneling, he'd reach into his carpenter's apron, pull out a nail and hammer it in. Every second or third nail that he pulled out and put against the panel, he'd look at it and then throw it away.

A puzzled Boudreaux asked, "Hey Shawee, why ya trowing dem nail away like dat?"

"Maaaaay, cuz dey no good!" said Shawee.

"May how come ya say dat?" questioned Boudreaux.

"Cuz da haid o' da nail is flat against da wall and da point is facing at me," replied Shawee. "Dey no good!"

"Sha Lawd. You stoopid yeah, you. Dem nail is fo' da opposite wall!" exclaimed Boudreaux.

Unwilling Hero

An oil well was on fire and burning out of control. So the rig foreman, T-Claude, decided to call Red Adair, the famous fire-fighter from Houston. Upon learning that Adair's fee was one million dollars to extinguish the blaze, he realized that it was too expensive and would have to look elsewhere. Browsing through the yellow pages, he came upon the firm of Red Boudreaux and Associates, Fire-Fighters Extraordinaire.

T-Claude called Boudreaux and inquired about his fee. Twenty thousand dollars seemed reasonable enough so he was asked to come immediately.

T-Claude was anxiously awaiting Boudreaux's arrival. At a distance he could see Boudreaux's old truck coming like a bat out of Hades, at a speed in excess of 100 MPH. The truck zoomed pass him and continued going toward the fire. The truck ran right through the fire and finally came to a halt. Boudreaux and his associate, Kymon, quickly jumped out of the truck and, with extinguishers and other special equipment, put out the fire.

T-Claude was amazed. He could hardly believe what he had seen. He told Boudreaux in a voice filled with excitement, "Man, dat's da mos bravest ting ah naver did see, me — running rat trew da fire like dat."

All Boudreaux could do was shake his head.

"Ya sho done a good job, you. But, lemme axe ya someting. Watchu gonna do wit all dat money ya jis made fo' yosef?" asked T-Claude.

"Huh, furst ting ahm goin' do, me, is git dem doggone brake fix!" exclaimed Boudreaux.

The Handy Man Can

Boudreaux was out of work and searched the neighborhood looking for odd jobs to pick up a few bucks. He came to a huge house, rang the doorbell and asked the owner if there was something he could do to earn some money.

"Sure," said an elderly lady. "Take this paint, go around the house and paint the porch."

A little while later Boudreaux returned. "Done already?" asked the lady.

"Haw yeah, beb!" said Boudreaux proudly. "But dat wudn't no porch, non, dat wuz a Mercedes!"

Best Laid Plans

A man from Houston, about to retire, decided to build a house in South Louisiana. He showed Boudreaux, a local carpenter, his plans and asked, "Can you build this?"

"Haaaaaw yeah!" said Boudreaux. "But ahm goin' told ya rat now — somebody done goofed up dese plans bad bad! But don't worry bot dat, dough. Ah kin draw ya up some new ones in a Sot Lafourche second."

"Look!" said the Texien. "I hired one of the top architectural firms in Houston to develop these blueprints. If you want the job, you'll follow these plans!"

"All rat, sha, no prablum," said Boudreaux. "But ahm tellin' ya. If ya use dese plans here, ya gonna wind up wit two batrums, yeah!"

For The Long Haul

Boudreaux went to the lumber yard and asked the salesman if he had any 2 x 4's on hand.

"How long do you need them?" asked the salesman as he pulled out a tape measure.

"Maaaaay, fo' a long, long time, sha," replied Boudreaux. "Cuz me dere, ahm building a new garage."

Better Late Than Never

Boudreaux had just started working at the paper mill in Valentine and had been caught coming in late three times already. On the fourth morning, the boss decided to read him the riot act.

"Look here, Boudreaux!" he snapped. "Don't you know what time we start work around here?"

"Ah sho don't, me," said Boudreaux, " cuz arrytime wen ah git here dey always working, dem."

Handle With Care

"Lemme give ya some good advice, Kymon." offered Boudreaux.

"May wats dat?" inquired Kymon.

"Don't naver buy nutting wit a hanal on it," said Boudreaux.

"How come?" asked Kymon.

"Cuz dat kin only mean some work!" explained Boudreaux.

Custom Made

Boudreaux opened a bicycle shop when the oil bust occurred. The economy was poor and jobs scarce.

T-Brud walked in and said, "Hey Boudreaux. Ah heard, me, datchu opened up dis bicycle shop, and ah jis wanted ta come see fo' mysef and ta see how ya doing. Kin ah look aroun' and see watchu got?"

"Haw yeah. Go 'head and make yosef at home, sha," said Boudreaux.

After browsing around for a few minutes T-Brud said, "Wait a minute dere, Boudreaux. Ya gotchu some bicycle here dat don't got no hanal bar and no seat. Dat don't make no sanse."

"May yeah," said Boudreaux. "Dat's fo' dem oil men dere dat lost so much dat dey don't kno ware ta sit and ware ta turn!"

Lights, Camera, Action!

Boudreaux was asked to play a part in a Hollywood movie. All he had to say was, "Hark, is that a cannon I hear?" He woke up early on the eventful morning and drove along Bayou Lafourche to the New Orleans airport. He made the connecting flight in Dallas and was on his way to Los Angeles. He must have practiced his line four or five thousand times enroute to Hollywood. "Hark, is that a cannon I hear?"

When he got on the set he was ready for his part. BOOM — the cannon went off. Boudreaux looked around in surprise and shouted, "May wat da heck wuz dat noise, sha?"

Lagniappe

If at this point you have determined that you are not a Cajun, don't be discouraged or depressed. There is still hope. You can be granted "Honorary Cajun" status; however, there are certain requirements to fulfill. In the presence of a group of bonafide Cajuns, you must:

1. Be able to tell a Boudreaux story in Cajun dialect.

2. Be able to locate Breaux Bridge, Mamou and Cut Off on the map without the use of a legend.

3. Be able to pronounce boscoyo and use it correctly in a sentence.

4. Be able to make a roux.

5. Be able to peel crawfish and eat them. Extra credit is given if you suck the heads.

6. Be able to pronounce Bourgeois, Arceneaux, Guilbeau, Theriot and Hebert.

7. Not be afraid if someone wants to axe you.

8. Be able to "pass a good time" anywhere at anytime.

9. Know which kind of cake contains the baby.

10. Attend a boucherie and be willing to taste boudin, hogshead cheese and gratons.

11. Be willing to yell iiiiieeeeeeeeeeeee in a public place at a moment's notice.

12. Have attended a three-pirogue wedding.

When you have successfully completed these conditions, the title of "Honorary Cajun" will be bestowed upon you and you will be entitled to all rights, privileges and honors of those who love the lifestyle of the Cajun people and culture. It doesn't get any better than this!

Summary

It is quite obvious by now that this endeavor was simply one of having fun. If there is a message at all it is that Cajuns enjoy life and living and make the most of every situation. We could all learn a lesson from this. A friend once gave me a button which read, "Enjoy life! This is not a dress rehearsal!" So true. Amidst all of our daily trials and tribulations, we must learn to look for and appreciate the humorous, even the ridiculous, events which can bring laughter to our lives. Unlike Boudreaux in the beer vat, we only go around once. So let's make the most of it, sha!

You may have noticed that this edition is called Volume 1 which indicates that there is more to come. You're right, there is! However, stories and anecdotes are needed in order for me to proceed. Therefore, I invite you to tap into your memory bank and recall all the Boudreaux stories you have deposited over the years. All printable stories are welcomed and can be sent to me via e-mail (curtboudreaux@cajunnet.com), fax (504-632-4898) or telephone (504-632-6177). I will gladly list you as a contributor in the next book. I look forward to hearing from you. Until then, MAKE yourself a great day and may God bless!

Glossary

aaaaaw - aw exaggerated
acta - actor
aducation - education
afta - after
aftanoon - afternoon
agin - again
ah - I
ahd - I'd
ahda - I would have
ahm - I'm
all riiiiight - all right
alrat - all right
alligata - alligator
alota - a lot of
alreddy - already
Anglish - English
annybody - anybody
ansa - answer
anudda - another
anvelope - envelope
aroun' - around
arr - air
arrpleen - airplane
arry - every
arrybody - everybody
arryone - everyone
arryting - everything
atall - at all
attantion - attention
aver - ever
aw - slang expression
axcuse - excuse
axe - ask
axercise - exercise

banka - banker
bartander - bartender
bat - bath
batrum - bathroom
battub - bath tub
beatchu - beat you
beb - baby
becuz - because
befo' - before
belief - believe
beliefed - believed
bert - birth
bess - best
bestest - best of all
betchu - bet you
bedda - better
bidness - business
bleave - believe
bote - both
bodda - bother
boondock - back woods *
boucherie - a communal butchering of swine or cattle to ensure a fresh supply of meat and by-products for the participants *
'bot - about
bottles - boggles
boudin - Cajun sausage *
Boudreaux - (Boo-drow)
bouray - (boo-ray) a Cajun card game in which the loser of the hand must match the take of the winning hand *
breade - breathe
Breaux Bridge - a small town in southwest Louisiana which hosts the Breaux Bridge Crawfish Festival annually *
breed - breathe
brudda - brother

* definition

bulleye - (boo-lie) a light that can be strapped to the forehead
and is used for hunting at night *

Bunkie - a small town in central Louisiana *

butchu - but you

butta - butter

Caaaaaw - slang used to express exitement or amazement, like
chooooo *

Cajun - a Louisianian who descends from French-speaking
Acadians. Also one from several ethnic groups over
which Acadian culture prevailed. *

camical - chemical

can'tchu - can't you

Catlic - Catholic

caw - car

'cept - except

chenged - changed

Chewsday - Tuesday

chockayed - incoherently drunk *

Chooooo - slang used to express excitement or amazement, like
caaaaaw *

clare - clear

cold cold - very cold

comin' - coming

computa - computer

condeaux - condo, condominium

convantion - convention

coss - cost

coupla - couple of

couyon - crazy *

Cowan - (cow-wan) turtle

crawfish - freshwater crustaceans resembling lobsters but
smaller in size. Sometimes called "mud bugs" *

'cross - across

* definition

crying up a storm - crying excessively hard *
cumpny - company
cuz - cause, because
da - the
dan - than
dat - that
datchu - that you
de - the
deat - death
dem - them
den - then, than
depand - depend
dere - there, their
dese - these
Desamba - December
didja - did you
din - didn't
dishwata - dishwater
dockta - doctor
doin' - doing
dolla(s) - dollar(s)
don'tchu - don't you
dough - though
down the bayou - headed south *
doze - those
dum - dumb
dummer - dumber
dunno - don't know
dy - thy
Easta - Easter
edda - either
enuff - enough
envie - (on-v) - a craving *
escalata - escalator
et - ate

* definition

etouffee - (ay-too-fay) - the ultimate cajun dish usually made with seafood in a smothered vegetable sauce *

exchenge - exchange

excitin' - exciting

expansive - expensive

Fabruary - February

fac - fact

Fadda - Father

fare - fair

fais-do-do - (fay-dough-dough) - a communal dance held traditionally in rural dancehalls. Children were put to sleep at the dances giving rise to the term, fais-do-do, meaning "go to sleep" in Cajun French. *

fas - fast

fava - favor

feva - fever

fella(s) - fellow(s)

fine - find

finga - finger

finely - finally

flo' - floor

fo' - four, for

foam - phone

fogot - forgot

fort - fourth, forth

foteen - fourteen

foth - fourth

fran - friend

frige - refrigerator

funral - funeral

furst - first

getta - get a

gill net - a monofilament net designed to catch fish by the gills *

gimme - give me

git - get

* definition

gitchu - get you
go head - go ahead
goin' - going
goooood - very good
gonna - going to
gotchu - got you
gotta - got to
gratons - hog cracklins; hog fat boiled in oil in a large black pot
        until crispy *
gulf - golf
gulfers - golfers
gumbo - a roux based soup of poultry, sausage or seafood
        served over rice *
haaaaaw - slang term used for emphasis *
hada - had a
hadna - had not
hadta - had to
haf - half, halve
hafta - have to
haid - head
haidache - headache
haidstone - headstone
hallo - hello
hanal - handle
hart - heart
havy - heavy
healt - health
'head - ahead
hep - help
histry - history
hmmmmmmmmmmmm - humming sound
hol - hold
holling - hollering
hoss - horse
hot cocoa - hot chocolate *

* definition

hot hot hot - extremely hot *
Hubba Hubba - a bar and cafe in Galliano owned and operated by the Cajun Ambassador, Emmanuel Toups (now closed) *
hurtchu - hurt you
idear - idea
imprassed - impressed
Innaneck - Internet
innastate - interstate
inta - into
intresting - interesting
invantion - invention
Januwary - January
jis - just
joie de vivre - joy of living *
Jolie Blonde - pretty blond *
Junya - Junior
kabooooom - slang term used to express a hit *
kin - can
kinda - kind of
kina - kind of
kinya - can you
Kymon - French for alligator *
laba - labor
laff - laugh
lagniappe - (lan-yap) - something extra *
Laissez Le Bon Temps Rouler - let the good times roll *
las - last
lawya - lawyer
Lawd - Lord
'lectric - electric
ledda - leather
lef - left
letchu - let you
letta - letter

* definition

lettus - let us
liberry - library
lika - like a
lil - little
looka - look at
loose - lose
lost bread - French toast *
lotta - lot of
lottry - lottery
lumba - lumber
luv - love
luvin' - loving
maaaaay - may
makin' - making
Mamou - a small town in southwestern Louisiana *
manny - many
Maree - (ma-ree - roll the r), Marie
matta - matter
may - but, well
minista - minister
mita - might have
mo' - more
moostache - mustache
mos - most
mornin' - morning
mout - mouth
muchu - much you
musta - must have
mysef - myself
na - now
naver - never
nedda - neither
neem - name
neighba - neighbor
nite - night

* definition

nombrie - navel *
non - no
nonk - uncle
Novamba - November
nowares - nowhere
nuff - enough
numba - number
nutting - nothing
o' - of
oat - oath
offen - often
okeration - operation
ole - old
oooooh - oh exaggerated
oppazit - opposite
orda - order
outa - out of
ova - over
ovahead - overhead
pacent - percent
Pagowww - to hit someone very hard *
pancil - pencil
pare - pair
Passova - Passover
pauvre bete - poor thing *
Pedro - a card game
peen - pain
Phideaux - Fido
pirogue - a small Cajun-styled boat similar to a canoe
pitcher - picture
planny - plenty
pleen - plain, plane
pleez - please
po' - poor
podna(s) - (pod-na(s)') partners, friends, companions

* definition

pooooo - an expression used to emphasize a point *
pooyie - (poo-yii) offensive *
posta - supposed to
prablemo - problem
prablum - problem
prancipal - principal
probly - probably
prod - proud
provida - provider
purty - pretty
put'em - put them
quarta - quarter
rat - right
recanize - recognize
reglar - regular
remamber - remember
restrunt - restaurant
round - around
roux - a flour and oil base used to make gumbo and gravy *
ruff - rough
Rumans - Romans
sacand - second
safa - safer
salabrate - celebrate
salabration - celebration
sand - send
sanse - sense
sant - sent
sants - cents
saven - seven
saventy - seventy
sax - sex
scheeeeeeeeeeeeee - a static sound *
scoop'em - scoop them
'scuse - excuse

* definition

seed - saw
seem - same
sefless steam - self-esteem
sha - cher, term of endearment *
shaaaaa - sha exaggerated *
shaka - shake a
shakin' - shaking
Shawee - French for racoon *
sho - show, sure
sista - sister
skool - school
sleaux - slow
slo - slow
smood - smooth
sooooo - so (exaggerated)
Sot Lafourche (South La-foosh) - a civil parish in southern
        Louisiana *
Sot Loseiana - South Louisiana
somewares - somewhere
sout - south
spackle trout - speckle trout
spand - spend
spant - spent
'spleen - explain
'spose - suppose
stap - step
stoopid - stupid
stoopidest - most stupid
strent - strength
sucka - sucker
suffa - suffer
sumo - some more
summa - summer
suppa - supper
swam - swim

* definition

swig - a sip

ta - to

Tabasco - a pepper sauce used to spice up many Louisiana
        recipes *

taday - today

tack - tact

talafoam - telephone

talavision - television

tamorra - tomorrow

tampermantal - tempermental

tan - ten

tank - thank

tankful - thankful

Tante - French for aunt *

taretened - threatened

tarrible - terrible

taut - thought

T-bebe (T-ba ba) - little baby *

Tchoupitoulas - (chop-i-to-lus) a street in New Orleans *

teacha - teacher

teree - three (roll the r)

tel - tell

tellya - tell you

termos - thermos bottle

tess - test

Texien - (Tex-e-en) a Texan *

three-pirogue wedding - the beer for a wedding reception is
        "iced down" in three pirogues. It is indicative of the size
        and length of the reception. *

tinking - thinking

tird - third

tirty - thirty

tirtiet - thirtieth

togedda - together

tolju - told you

* definition

tonite - tonight
toot - tooth
torns - thorns
tousand - thousand
traiteur - (tray-tur) a faith healer *
treens - trains
trew - through
troat - throat
troot - truth
trow - throw
tuff - tough
Tursday - Thursday
twanny-saven - twenty-seven
udda - other
unda - under
undastand - understand
undataka - undertaker
uuuuugly - very, very, very ugly *
usta - used to
varry - very
Wal-Mark - Wal-Mart
wamans - women
wanchu - want you
wanna - want to
wanta - want to
ware - wear, where
ware's - where's
waring - wearing
wat - what
wata - water
wataver - whatever
watchall - what yall
watchu - what you
weekan' - weekend

* definition

Weeza - Louise
wen - when
wert - worth
wetta - whether
whew - sigh of relief *
whol' - whole
whooop - wait a minute, hold on *
winda - window
winna - winner
wipa - wiper
winta - winter
wit - with
witchu - with you
witin - within
wonda - wonder
wooda - would have
woodju - would you
worser - worse than the other
worstest - the worse of all
wrasslin' - wrestling
wrat - write
writin' - writing
wudn't - wasn't
wuz - was
wuzn't - wasn't
yabbut - yes but
yea - yes
yeah - yes
yestiddy - yesterday
yo' - your
ya - you, your
zackly - exactly

* definition

Bibliography

Conrad, Glenn (Editor). The Cajuns: Essays On Their History And Culture. Lafayette, LA: Center For Louisiana Studies, 1978.

Woolfork, Doug (Publishing Editor). The Longest Street. Baton Rouge, LA: Moran Publishing Corporation, 1980.

About The Author

Curt Boudreaux is a professional speaker and author. He received a B.S. from Nicholls State University in Thibodaux, Louisiana and a Masters +30 degree in Guidance and Counseling from Ole Miss.

He was an educator for twenty-four years and served as principal of Golden Meadow Middle School for ten. In 1988 he was honored as a National Distinguished Principal. This award is jointly sponsored by the U.S. Department of Education and the National Association of Elementary School Principals to recognize excellence in school administration. Only one public school principal from each state is selected annually for this award.

Curt is a member of the National Speakers Association and past president of the New Orleans Chapter. He is also past Chairman of the Board of the South Lafourche Chamber of Commerce and past Chairman of the Board of Commissioners of Lady of the Sea Hospital.

He is a twelve year veteran of prison ministry work and is a volunteer in the Kairos Prison Ministry at Louisiana State Penitentiary at Angola.

Curt retired from education nine years ago to pursue a career in professional speaking. He gives keynotes, seminars and workshops throughout the country addressing the topics of self-esteem, attitude, human relations and now, Cajun humor. Check out his web site at www.nolaspeaks.com/cb .

He is the author of the book The ABC's of Self-Esteem and has recorded an audio tape entitled "The Keys To Unlocking Your Potential."

Curt works with individuals who want to improve the

quality of their lives and with companies and organizations that want their people to develop their potential. His sense of humor, enthusiasm and passion for speaking combined with strong presentation skills enable him to relate easily to audiences and effectively communicate his message.

Curt and his wife, Sue, live in the small community of Cut Off, Louisiana, along the banks of Bayou Lafourche. This Cajun speaks from the heart! Let him speak to yours! Should you be interested in Curt speaking to your group or ordering products, you may contact him at:

Synergy Press
Curt Boudreaux
P.O. Box 422
Golden Meadow, Louisiana 70357

504-632-6177 - Telephone
504-632-4898 - Fax
curtboudreaux@cajunnet.com - e-mail

Programs

Never Kiss An Alligator On The Lips!

An entertaining talk, it centers on Cajun humor featuring the legendary stories of Boudreaux, the Cajun. It includes some "you just might be a Cajun if" thoughts and is ideal for banquets and after dinner humor.

The ABC's of Self-Esteem

Attitude, belief and confidence are discussed and their relation to building self-esteem. Participants are allowed to select areas of interests from the remaining twenty-three topic words. This talk corresponds to his book by the same title.

The Keys To Unlocking Your Potential

The focus of this talk is to dream big dreams, believe in oneself and take positive risks. It also relates to his audio tape. It is practical as well as inspirational and encourages participants to be all they can be.

The Human Side of Quality

This talk addresses improving the individual or employee through personal and interpersonal development as opposed to increasing their technical skills. The essence of self-esteem, human relations and communication are examined and discussed.

You Only Go Around Once!

This inspirational talk is designed to encourage individuals to "go for it!" Rising above temporary defeat, being inspired, having courage and a zest for living are among the issues presented. It is laced with liberal doses of humor and is highly motivational.

The Art of Leadership
Effective leadership is crucial in many aspects of personal and professional life. Insights for improving leadership skills are viewed with an eye on qualities of a leader, leadership practices, myths and realities, also the leader versus the non-leader.

Winning Attitudes
As much as eighty-five percent of a person's success can be attributed to attitude. Participants come to grips with the importance of believing in oneself, having self-confidence, setting-goals and having high expectations. Possession of these attitudes can propel a person into the winner's circle.

KING CAKE

Product Order Form

Never Kiss An Alligator On The Lips! (Book)
Price: $20.00 (Louisiana residents add $1.50 sales tax per book)* Add postage/shipping costs at the rate of $2.00 for the first book and $1.00 for each additional book.

The ABC's of Self-Esteem: A Practical Approach (Book)
Price: $20.00 (Louisiana residents add $1.50 sales tax per book)* Add postage/shipping costs at the rate of $2.00 for the first book and $1.00 for each additional book.

"The Keys To Unlocking Your Potential" (Audio tape)
Price: $10.00 (Louisiana residents add $.75 sales tax per tape)* Add postage/shipping costs at the rate of $1.00 for the first tape and $.50 for each additional tape.

"ABC's of Self-Esteem" (Poster) 18 X 24 four color
Price: $7.00 (Louisiana residents add $.50 sales tax per poster)* Add $3.00 for postage/shipping costs for the first 5 posters and $.50 for every additional 5 posters.

_____ **Never Kiss An Alligator On The Lips!**
@ $20.00 + $1.50 tax per book _____
Postage/shipping costs _____

_____ **The ABC's of Self-Esteem (Book)**
@ $20.00 + $1.50 tax per book _____
Postage/shipping costs _____

_____ **"The Keys To Unlocking Your Potential"**
@ $10.00 + $.75 tax per tape _____
Postage/shipping costs _____

_____ **"ABC's of Self-Esteem" (Poster)**
@ $7.00 + $.50 tax per poster _____
Postage/shipping costs _____

Total Amount Due _____

*Schools/school districts are tax exempt

Make check or money order payable to
Curt Boudreaux and mail to:

Curt Boudreaux, P.O. Box 422, Golden Meadow, LA 70357

Phone (504-632-6177) • Fax (504-632-4898)
E-mail (curtboudreaux@cajunnet.com)

****

Name _____

Telephone (_____) _____

Address _____

_____

City _____State _____Zip _____

****

Web site: www.nolaspeaks.com/cb

_____ Please send details about Curt Boudreaux speaking to
my group.